Timothy

His Protectors

Book 1

By

Ronna M. Bacon

Deuteronomy 31:6 Be strong and of a good courage, fear not, nor be afraid of them: for the LORD your God, he it is that does go with you; he will not fail you, nor forsake you.

Psalms 57:1. 1 Have mercy on me, my God, have mercy on me, for in you I take refuge. I will take refuge in the shadow of your wings until the disaster has passed.

NKJV

Table of Contents

Sitting back on his heels, Timothy Steele stared down at his hands, hands that were bracing him upright as they rested on his thighs. They were battered, cut, and bruised, scraped as well. He tried to draw in a deep breath, the pain from his ribs keeping him from doing that. He squinted as he glanced up at the noon-time sun, the brightness hurting his eyes and causing the headache to become even more intense. His head dropped once more as he struggled to breathe. He staggered to his feet, waiting for his head to clear. Timothy bent to retrieve the backpack that had been thrown beside him, his head spinning as he did so. He staggered sideways for a moment, his eyes closing against the whirling in front of his eyes.

Timothy drew in a deep breath, his eyes searching the small crowd that had gathered around him. The men who had assaulted him seemed to have disappeared, he decided. He was at a loss to know why he had been approached like that. The men had simply stood in his way, not moving even as he had stopped.

"Excuse me?" Timothy had waited for either of the men to speak or at least step to one side.

Neither man moved or spoke. They just stood there, staring at Timothy.

Timothy sighed to himself. He was off for the next week and had planned to spend it hiking during the day in his home area. That seemed not to be the case today.

"Excuse me? I would like to pass, if I may." Timothy waited for a moment and then moved to go around him. Only he didn't make it.

The taller of the men raised a hand and stopped Timothy in his tracks. The hand rested on Timothy's shoulder.

Timothy shrugged to try and remove it but that didn't work. He drew in a deep breath, having a feeling that something bad was about to go down. And that worried him, a lot. He worked for a security team and had never felt as he did at that point. Timothy saw the fist heading his way and tried to dodge him, his arm coming up to block it. As he did that, the second man's fist landed on his abdomen, driving the breath from him. He staggered backwards, not willing to go down. He had no chance against his two assailants and finally was driven to the ground.

The men had stared down at him and then walked away. Their work was done. They had been told to find Timothy and stop him. They didn't need to know why.

Timothy had finally managed to raise himself up, to sit back on his legs. That had taken some work. Not one person had offered to help him and he frowned at that. This was not his town, not at all.

He stood for a moment, assessing the mood of the crowd, deciding that he was safe for now. He searched further and his eyes stopped on a young lady who stood in the crowd. She was about his age, he decided, taking in the red gold hair that curled around her face and down her shoulders. He walked towards her, surprised that she didn't look up as he stood in front of her.

Frowning, Timothy turned somewhat, his eyes on the crowd. He could see some of them had left but a number were still there watching him. He sighed. *Now what, Lord? Where do I go from here? I can't walk away from this lady. I don't know her. At least I don't think that I do, but she is in trouble. I can sense that. And it seems that You have placed me here to help her.*

Timothy reached for her hand, finding hers cold and limp. He frowned once more as his own hand tightened on hers. He turned again to study the people there, finding not one watching him but watching the area around him. That genuinely puzzled him. Turning back to the lady, he caught the look of fear in her amber eyes. He frowned deeper before he turned, walking away, her hand still in his. She kept step with him but just barely.

Rubbing at his face, Timothy grimaced with pain as he felt the bruises and scrapes on it. His hand went to his dark blond hair, knowing that it was tousled and dirty. His deep gray eyes searched for someone who meant him harm but no one stood out.

Finding somewhere to sit at last, Timothy drew the lady down with him. He watched her closely, assessing her without saying a word.

"My name is Timothy. I won't hurt you. But I would like to know your name." He waited, patiently, knowing that when someone was deep in fear, it might take a long time to respond.

The lady spoke at last, her voice barely audible.

"I'm Tate. Tate Talbot. Are you okay?" She didn't look at him.

His head tilting slightly to see her face, Timothy nodded. She was afraid, he thought. Just why that was he was determined to find out.

"Not really." Timothy didn't want to admit how much he was hurting and knew that he would be even sorer by the next day. "You're in trouble."

Tate simply shook her head. She was afraid, she admitted to herself. Only no one would help her. She had no one to turn to. Her family had turned their backs on her. She didn't understand why. Tate knew that she had been followed for weeks now. The men were overt in their stalking of her. She saw them every day, everywhere she went.

"I'm not. But you can't help. No one can."

The resignation in her voice tugged at Timothy. It was not in him to walk away from anyone, not in his character or in his line of work. He was certain that God had placed him there. He just didn't know why he had been beaten as much as he had. It didn't make sense.

Timothy looked around, sensing someone watching him or watching Tate. He wasn't sure which one of them was under observation. And it wasn't for their health, he decided. He was on his feet, watching Tate's face. He reached for her hand once more, drawing her to her feet. He bit back groans as the pain hit harder and in deeper waves. He needed to get them to safety. Just how he was going to do that, he had no idea.

Tate looked up at last, way up, she thought. The man with her was tall. She was afraid for him. He had come to her aid and that she thought would not go over well with whoever it was after her.

"Tate? Are you on the run?" Timothy finally had to ask her that.

Tate hesitated before she nodded.

"I am. Only I don't know why." She looked around, searching for whoever it was that she could feel.

"Okay." Timothy's steps were slowing as the pain hit harder and harder. It was making it difficult to see. He dropped to his knees, arms wrapping around his abdomen, unable to keep the groan from tearing from his body.

Tate stood, hands over her mouth, before she was on her knees beside him. He was hurt because of her, she felt. But how did she get him to help?

Neither one of them heard the quiet footsteps that approached or the quiet words that were spoken. Tate was drawn to her feet, an arm around her even as two men bent to help Timothy to his own feet.

Richard, Timothy's team leader, watched him closely. Someone from the area had reached out to him, sending him on a search. Stephen, Silver, and Naomi, the other three on his team, had been shocked to hear that Timothy was in danger but had willingly and gladly dropped their plans for that Saturday and rushed to help.   An ambulance approached, the paramedics reaching for Timothy.

Timothy roused for a moment, searching for Tate, a hand out for hers. He refused to drop it even as he drifted back into that well of unconsciousness. His team members stared at the couple before they exchanged glances.

Just what is going on, Richard wondered. This is not Timothy. Not to do this. And they had no idea how he had been hurt or why. The caller had simply told Richard that Timothy needed help and where to find him.

Chapter 2

Tate sat silently in the hospital waiting room. Her gaze was directed at the floor, not paying attention to anyone around her. Silver sat beside her, watching between Tate and Richard. She knew her other two teammates, Stephen and Naomi, were around somewhere. Richard in turn watched Tate, not sure at all who she was or how she ended up with Timothy. He would need to speak with Timothy. Only he was told that wouldn't be happening, not yet at any point. Timothy was unconscious and would be that way for a while from what the physician had said. And did Richard know his family, so that they could be called? Richard had simply nodded and moved away to make that phone call. Timothy's brother, Nathan, had answered, surprised to hear from Richard.

"Richard? What's up?" Nathan turned from watching his young son playing with the young puppy that had just joined their home.

"Nathan? I'm here at the hospital with Timothy." Richard turned back to keep an eye on Tate.

"The hospital? What happened? He was off this week, just planning on doing some hiking in the area." Nathan was on his feet, heading for where his wife was working in the gardens.

"I don't know the whole story. He was found earlier, severely beaten. The thing of it is that there was a young lady with him. By the name of Tate. Do you know her?"

"Tate? No, that's not a name that I recognize." Nathan briefly moved his phone to let his wife know what was going on. "I'm on my way in, Richard. Call me if there is any update."

Richard pocketed his phone, his eyes on Tate. He gave a soft sound and was rapidly at her side. He had watched Tate as her eyes closed and her head went back against the wall. He gathered her into his arms and rapidly walked towards the exam rooms. The clerk took one look and then hit the security switch to open the door for him.

The charge nurse pointed him towards an exam room. Richard gently laid Tate on the stretcher and then stepped back. He motioned to Silver to remain with her. He walked away, looking for Stephen.

Stephen turned from where he had been watching the room where the physician was working on Timothy.

"Stephen? What's the word?" Richard cared deeply about his team, first as a co-worker and then as a friend. His heart raised in prayer for Timothy.

"He's still out of it, Richard. We haven't been able to get any information from him. I talked to Bill as well. He was around. He's been through the area where we found them. No one is saying anything." Stephen was puzzled by that.

"They're scared and scared badly. I spoke with Nathan. He's on his way in."

"I figured that he would be. How's Tate?" Stephen had watched as Richard had carried her back to the room.

"She's out of it as well. I have no idea what is going on. And I'm not sure if she'll tell us." Richard walked away on that, his phone out. "Bill? Where are you?"

"Right behind you." Bill walked towards Richard, a frown on his face. "What's going on?"

"I wish I knew. And that is a fact." Richard pointed towards the doors. "Let's walk. I'll tell you what I know and it's not that much after all."

Richard and Bill spoke for a while, neither of them having any answers as to what happened. Bill Buckley, a detective with the Elmton force, watched as Richard walked away, his steps heavy. This was not how he had planned to spend his Saturday, Bill knew.

Bill sighed. Was another friend about to undergo one of those adventures that he and others of their friends had? He stared up at the bright blue sky, his thoughts troubled and muddled. *God, You are here. You have allowed this. Protect our friend. Let us resolve this without any further harm to Timothy and Tate. Only, somehow I don't think that will happen.*

Naomi approached Bill, a puzzled look on her face.

"Bill? What do you know?" She stopped beside him, her arms wrapped around herself. This had upset the whole team. Not once had this happened to them, at least, not for one of them.

<hr>

"Not a lot, Naomi. Did you notice anything?" Bill knew that Richard had trained his team well to be observant.

"Not really, Bill. There was a group of around ten to twelve around them. They were standing back from Timothy.   I think there may have been an undercover officer there. Just an impression that I got." Naomi was troubled at not knowing much.

"That's okay, Naomi. We're canvassing the area, looking for anyone who can help. There aren't any cameras in that area." Bill walked away, heading for the detachment and his fellow officers, hoping that someone had found the culprits and didn't really think that had happened.

Naomi found Stephen, standing side by side with him. They didn't speak. They didn't have to, they had worked together for years. Both were deep in prayer, worried about their friend and worried about the danger that he had found himself involved in.

Timothy had begun to rouse, his head tossing restlessly against the pillow. The physician watched him before he spoke to Nathan.

"Your brother is fortunate, Nathan. It could have been a lot worse. No broken bones. No internal injuries. Whoever did this made sure that he was harmed but not to the point that he was in life threatening condition."

"That's what is puzzling me, Rod. Who did this?" Nathan was worried, more worried than he had been for a long while. He and Timothy had spoken many times about Timothy's work. Timothy usually was offhand about what danger he faced, not too open with his brother. None of his team was.

"Find them, Nathan. He might not survive if it happens again. He does have a concussion. I'll speak with Richard if that's okay." Rod walked away, finding Richard waiting for him.

"Rod?" Richard looked at him and then back into the room, watching as Nathan moved closer to his brother, his hands on the side rail of the stretcher.

"He has a concussion, Richard, and won't be working for at least ten days or more. That affects your team. Other than that, he'll be sore. No broken bones. No internal injuries. I would suggest that whoever did this was a professional. Now, about the lady who you said was with him?"

"Tate?" Richard turned that way. "We don't know anything about her."

"That's what the nurse said. I see Silver is with her. That's fine. What can you tell me?"

"Nothing, other than her name. That's all she would give us. Bill investigating her but he didn't know if he'd find out a whole lot yet." Richard paused in the doorway, a frown on his face.

Tate was awake, standing by the stretcher, absolute terror on her face. Her gaze shot between the three of them before she was on the run, searching for someone. Only she didn't know who she was searching for. She slid to a stop as she saw Stephen and then heard Nathan's voice. As Nathan moved slightly, she saw Timothy. *He can keep me safe,* she thought. *I need to stay with him. He'll figure out why those men took me. Only, I don't know how safe I will be. And I don't know why they took me. God, You promised to protect me, to provide a safe haven. I could use that about now, God.*

Chapter 3

Nathan spun as he heard hurried footsteps heading his way, a frown on his face as he saw the lady almost running towards Timothy. He reached out a hand to stop her. Only, she dodged him and slid to a halt on the other side of the stretcher. Nathan frowned deeper. He didn't know who this was and why she was there.

Richard had followed Silver into the room. Silver had quickly moved to Tate's side, Richard pausing at the end of the stretcher. There were too many people in the room, he knew, but he had no idea how to remove Tate other than to bodily pick her up and carry her away. That was something he was prepared to do, if necessary, but the look on Tate's face stopped him. He shared a look with Silver who simply shrugged.

Timothy's eyes flickered open and he groaned as the light hit them. A hand went up to cover them. Nathan waited for Timothy to speak, knowing that his brother would when he was able to. His eyes went to Tate, watching her closely. He didn't know her, he knew. His gaze shifted to Silver, watching Silver instead. He could tell how intense she was watching Tate.

Tate stood for a moment before she reached for Timothy's hand, hers cold on his. She felt him jump slightly as she touched him. She prayed that he would be all right, not sure why he had been beaten. She didn't think it was related to her but she didn't know that for sure. She was just so exhausted and wanted to sleep. That couldn't happen, not yet, she knew. Her eyes raised and she frowned at Nathan as he stared at her before she looked back down at Timothy.

Rousing further, Timothy had stared around, not moving his head, knowing that his headache would only worsen. He acknowledged Richard as his boss stood at the end of the bed, watching Tate instead of him. Silver next came under his contemplation. He knew that his brother was standing beside him. He had heard him speaking to him not that long ago.

His head turned slightly and then stopped. Another lady was standing there, one who he didn't know. It was her hand on his. This was not him, to have a lady doing this. Well, other than his mother or his brother's wife, Shari. He licked at his lips but before he could speak, his eyes closed and he slept.

Richard moved to stand on the other side of Tate, not sure what to say.

"Tate?" Richard's voice was quiet, just loud enough for Tate to hear.

Tate jumped, her eyes huge with fright as she stared up at him.

"Who are you? And where am I?" Tate spun, staring at Silver and then at Nathan.

"I'm Richard. That's Silver beside you. And the man across from you is Timothy's brother, Nathan. And your name is Tate? Correct?"

Tate nodded at last, her eyes not moving from Richard.

"I don't understand. Where am I? I don't know this place?"

"You're in the hospital in Elmton. We found you just outside of town. I don't think that this is where you're from." Richard saw Bill hesitating in the doorway, not entering, merely nodding for Richard to continue.

"No, I'm not. I'm from.." Tate's voice dropped off. "I'm not from here. I don't know that I should tell you where I'm from. I don't know you."

Richard grinned for a moment, causing her to frown at him even harder.

"That's fair. I don't know you either but I would like to. Timothy seems to think that you need our help. And we can assist you with that."

Tate felt a hand on hers and looked down. Timothy had roused once more, finding Tate not looking at him. His hand had slipped out from under hers and then laid on top of hers.

"It's okay. He's right. We will help." Timothy had trouble speaking, the headache causing him to squint against the light.

"You're awake?" Tate frowned at him even harder, thinking that was all she was doing that day.

"I am. Nathan, when can I leave?"

Nathan shook his head, knowing that Timothy would just refuse to stay in the hospital but he wasn't well enough to be on his own.

"In the next while. And you're not heading for your home. You're either with me or with Richard or Stephen. That's the only way you can leave." Nathan shared another look with Richard.

"I guess. How soon?"

Rod walked towards the group, eyeing each one.

"Timothy? I need to examine you. Everyone here has to leave." Rod bit back a smile as Timothy's hand tightened on Tate's. "It's okay, Timothy. Your lady will be safe and will be right outside the door. Nathan? He's going to your place? Then, you stay."

Tate shifted from foot to foot, anxiety in her very bearing. Silver stood close to her, her eyes moving around. Richard had moved away to speak with Bill.

"Bill? Where are we to put Tate? She's not from here." Richard was worried. His work as a security team head had him running all the scenarios that he could think of.

"No, she's not. Your team is away next week, I know. I don't think that she's willing to walk away from Timothy. She seems to feel responsible for him being hurt." Bill had done some investigating and knew that at some point he would need to interview Tate.

"I think she is but I have no proof of that." Richard turned to head back for the room, Bill pacing beside him.

Tate almost ran back towards Timothy, finding him standing by the stretcher, unsteady on his feet.

"Timothy! You shouldn't be standing. You're going to fall." Tate tried her best to make him sit back down.

Timothy simply wrapped her in his arms, startling her and bringing looks from the others. This was not Timothy. He shook his head at Nathan before meeting Bill's eyes. He knew that he would need to give a statement. Only he had no idea what kind of a statement to give.

His heart began to pray, asking for peace and safety for his lady. He prayed earnestly for Tate, knowing that somehow their lives had become entwined and that they would be endangered until they could solve whatever it was.

Nathan's hand went out as did Richard's. They directed Timothy to a wheel chair, grinning as Tate's hands reached for the handles

"Where to, Timothy?" Nathan waited for Timothy to make his own decision.

Timothy sighed, his head pounding and his other injuries beginning to hurt more than he expected.

"Your place, I guess. Tate comes with me." He didn't see Tate's look of shock and her beginning to shake her head. "We have to, Tate. We need to keep you safe. Only I'm not sure from what."

Chapter 4

Shari walked through their house, mugs of tea in her hand, heading for the back patio. She knew that Tate was out there, the other lady refusing to enter their home. Shari wasn't sure why that was but she knew that she would convince her at some point to do so. Silver and Naomi were around, she knew, the two ladies have done a shopping run and brought clothes and whatever else was needed for Tate.

Tate looked up in fear, reaching for the mug that Shari held out. She didn't understand why she was so afraid. She couldn't understand it.

Richard was around, deep in discussion with Nathan. Nathan was a firefighter and had bluntly asked Richard what they could do to help.

Timothy had stretched out on a lounge on the back patio. He just didn't have the energy to move any further. Besides, he knew that Tate was close by and that was what he wanted. He began to pray once more, seeking safety for the lady who had invaded his life. He didn't realize that she was bringing danger to him, more danger than he had ever faced in his work. Timothy wouldn't have cared if he had known. His whole purpose in life was keeping others safe and that now included Tate.

Shari waited for Tate to speak, content to sit in the warmth of the day. Their son wandered around before he crawled up beside his uncle, cuddling down under Timothy's arm and drifted off to sleep.

Tate yawned, fatigue hitting her hard. She could barely keep her eyes open but didn't want to sleep. She was sure that Timothy would disappear if she did sleep and she needed to talk with him. Shari watched with compassion before she was on her feet, drawing Tate to hers and then with an arm around her, directing her into the house and to the conservatory. Tate stared in awe at the room before Shari had gently shoved her to a couch, reaching to draw the other lady's feet up and then draping a blanket over her.

"Have a sleep, Tate. You're safe here. When you awaken, then I'll show you the room that you can use. It has an attached bathroom. Silver and Naomi went shopping for you and the bags are in the room. You'll want to clean up."

Shari gave a sad smile as she stood in the doorway, her eyes on Tate. She felt Nathan's arms around her.

"They're both sleeping?"

Shari nodded.

"Timothy is asleep on the patio. Tate could barely stay awake. What's her story?" Shari walked towards the kitchen, Nathan following. "And little Ben is asleep with his uncle."

"I wondered where he was. Richard is off for now but he'll be back. Silver and Naomi are here for now. They said that they weren't leaving. Stephen is off with Richard. I am not sure what they are up to."

"Looking into Tate, I would suspect." Shari reached for food from the fridge. "I'll make up some sandwiches for lunch. I have soup that I can heat for Timothy. He'll not want a lot."

"No, he won't." Nathan reached for the loaves of bread that Shari had in her hands. "He'll sleep a lot. We need to wake him every couple of hours."

"And that won't go over well." Shari paused as she was slicing tomatoes, the knife held above one. "God is here, Nathan. I can feel Him. I just wish that Timothy was not in danger."

"He's in danger all the time, love. It's his job." Nathan worked away at buttering the bread and then placing the meat on it. He turned to the fridge for the sliced cheese.

"I know that he is. This is different. This is directed at him. Do we know what happened?" Shari turned to her husband, finding him reaching to hug her.

"No, I don't know that we do. He was beaten and from what little Richard has determined had somehow fixated on Tate and was trying to get away with her. That's when he collapsed." Nathan just held his wife, feeling her fear for her beloved brother-in-law. "God is in control. We know that. This is when it will be hard to trust Him completely and fully. And we'll need to. Timothy will do everything he can to keep you and Ben safe."

"I know that he will but will it be enough?" Shari moved away from him, reaching for plates and utensils, setting them on a tray. She opened the fridge to stare into it, sorting out in her mind what they had in cold sodas and juice.

———

"Whatever we offer them will do, love." Nathan grinned as she frowned at him. "It's not the first time that we have shared a meal with Richard and his team. And it won't be the last. I understand that Bill is planning on dropping by later and that Cora and Michael will be with him."

"They will? Ok, good. Ben loves playing with little Michael. I think they're best friends."

"I think so too." Nathan turned as he heard shuffled footsteps and Timothy appeared, Ben in his arms. "Timothy?"

"Nathan? What's going on? Why am I here?" Timothy was confused, forgetting what had happened. "I hurt, all over."

"You were beaten, Timothy." Shari reached for her son, motioning to Nathan. "Go on. Nathan dropped by your place and grabbed some clothes for you. Go and get cleaned up. Then I have some food for you."

Timothy barely nodded, moving past them and to the hallway, heading for the room where he knew he would find his clothes. Nathan and Shari had a large rambling one-storey home, with five bedrooms. They were always willing to help someone out for a few days.

Nathan kept a close eye on his brother, not sure if Timothy should be on his feet, but knowing his brother well enough to know that Timothy would be up and around even if he wasn't able to and shouldn't have been.

"Tate's sleeping in the conservatory. Bill's on his way over."

"Tate? Who's she? And why would Bill be heading this way?" Timothy simply grabbed clean clothes and shut the bathroom door behind him. He stared at his face, shocked at the bruising and knowing that while the hot water would help soothe the hurt, it would also hurt.

Nathan shook his head. It was about what he figured would happen. Timothy had forgotten what had happened and that they didn't need. He was about the only one who could describe who had assaulted him and whether something had been said to him.

Chapter 5

Tate roused late in the afternoon, snuggling down under the blanket. She lay there, her senses letting her know that she wasn't in her own home. She didn't know where she was but she felt safe. Jumping slightly as she felt tiny fingers prying at her eyelids, Tate smiled and then opened her eyes. Little Michael was there, his face close to hers, his fingers on her cheeks.

"Hello, there." Tate's voice was soft, startling Michael for a moment.

"You awake?" Michael's head was nodding, a grin on his face. "Up. Food."

"There's food? Can I have some?" Tate sat up, reaching for Michael and cuddling him close. He snuggled back, forgetting that he had mentioned food.

Cora and Shari had come looking for Michael, pausing as they saw Tate holding Michael with Ben struggling to get up beside her.

"Tate? You're awake." Shari moved towards her, sitting beside her and lifting Ben up, who promptly hugged Tate. "I think that you have some friends here."

Tate nodded, catching sight of Cora.

"I'm sorry, I don't know you." She looked down at Michael. "This is your son?"

"That's Michael. I'm Cora. I think my husband, Bill, will be speaking with you. He's a police detective

---

29

here, the chief detective in fact. If not today, then early next week.”

“Today I think. Then, I need to find a ride home. I can’t stay here.” Tate grew pensive and sad.

“You can, Tate. You are more than welcome to say here. In fact, Bill would like that.” Shari reached out to give her a one-armed hug. “What about your family?”

“My family? The ones who deserted me years ago and told me that I wasn’t worth their time? That family?” Tate had grown resigned to her family’s hatred even if she didn’t understand why.

“That’s so sad, Tate. We want to be friends with you, if you’ll let us. We have a group of ladies that meet for Bible study and prayer. You would be welcome.” Shari looked around as she heard footsteps. “And here’s Phoebe. Phoebe, meet Tate. Tate, Phoebe is a dear friend but is also the wife of our police chief.”

“Hi.” Tate grew shy, not sure about anything anymore.

Phoebe watched with compassion.

“It’s hard, isn’t it, Tate? I’m not from this town. Andrew and I married one day after he rescued me. Not that I recommend that for every couple. We are deeply in love. Some day, I’ll share our story and Cora will share hers and Bill’s.”

Tate nodded, sure that she would be gone before that happened. She was on her feet, her hands in Michael’s and Ben’s as the two little fellows led her towards the kitchen and then the back patio. She blinked at the bright light, sensing someone near her. Tate looked up to find Timothy beside her. His face was bruised and battered and she could see the pain that he was trying hard to hide in the clenched jaw and in his eyes.

"Timothy? You shouldn't be standing." Tate couldn't free her hands. As she tried, the little fellows just tightened their grip on hers.

"I'm sorry? Do I know you?" Timothy thought that he should but he wasn't sure.

"Know me? Just what do you mean?" Tate didn't understand. She looked down at the little faces looking up at her and then moved away, greeting Richard and the ladies and then being introduced to Bill and Andrew.

Nathan stopped beside his brother, a smirk on his face.

"Can't remember her? But you want to?" He laughed at the glare sent his way. "You know her, my brother. Only we don't know why. Or who is was that beat you up. We're not sure either if it's all related."

"I see." Timothy looked around for a chair, ready to sit before he fell. His strength wasn't what it usually was.

Richard and Andrew had moved in, their hands out to keep him steady. They shared a glance before Richard sighed and spoke.

"We need to get you sitting down, Timothy. We'll talk tomorrow. And I know that it's Sunday. Silas and Madison are aware of what happened and will be around tomorrow afternoon. You won't feel like going tomorrow."

Timothy nodded and then regretted it, his eyes squeezing shut against the pain. He felt a hand on his and then a hand resting on his cheek. His eyes opened to find Tate on her knees beside his chair, worry on her face.

"Timothy? You need to rest. You have a concussion." Worry laced her words.

"I know I do. But I need to know who you are and why you're here. I don't understand that."

Tate was on her feet, her face shuttering. She turned and almost ran from the patio, her feet flying through the house and out of the front door. She had disappeared before any of the men could react.

They searched for her, not finding her. Andrew and Bill had called in officers to help search, to no avail.

Timothy had collapsed again, the pain too much. He had been helped back to his bed by Richard and Nathan, Shari watching closely. The other two ladies had stared at one another before they had bowed their heads to pray. Silver and Naomi had taken off in Silver's car, driving slowly through the neighbourhood.

"Where would she go, Silver?" Naomi was worried. She had liked what she had seen of Tate and wanted to get to know her better, to make her a friend.

"I don't know." Silver pulled to a stop at the curb, thinking through the area. "The park? The one not far from here? Would she go there?"

No one had found Tate, despite searching for her. Timothy had not roused to the point that Nathan had taken him back to the hospital where he was admitted. Bill was concerned about Tate, heading to the streets to search for her. No one had seen her or so they said. Bill sat in his car, his eyes on an abandoned building nearby. *Where is she, Lord? We need to find her. Only we can't. She's in Your hands, the best place to be. Only she'll need our help.*

Chapter 6

A week had passed. Timothy had healed as much as he could but was still restricted from working because of his concussion. This bothered him greatly. He felt as if he was letting his team down but Richard had finally turned to him, simply telling him that he needed to heal. They would manage. He could work in the office, dealing with that instead of Richard doing it after-hours or on weekends. Timothy had grumbled, Richard grinning at that, and agreed.

He had searched the town himself, looking for Tate. He had asked everyone he could ask if they had seen her. Some had hesitated before they shook their heads. They had walked after him as he walked away, knowing where Tate was but knowing that she didn't want to have Timothy find her.

Tate had watched him that last morning, a week after the attack, her steps taking her on a path that followed him and led her to his home. She sat on the porch steps of his neighbour across the street, not caring at that point if anyone saw her.

The older lady stood at her open door, a frown on her face. She watched Tate for a moment before she came out and just sat beside her. She was a retired officer and knew how to read people. She could tell that Tate was troubled.

Tate jumped as she sensed someone sit beside her. She sighed. She gathered up what strength she had and made a move to step. A hand on her arm stopped her. Tate stared across the street at Timothy's

—

34

house. She didn't want to see him hurt again but she did desperately need to talk with him. She just didn't know how to go about that.

Mae Thomas sat beside Tate, not saying anything for a moment. She had a good idea who the lady was, the friend of Timothy who went missing the week before.

"It's okay. I know that you're Timothy's friend. Aren't you?" She waited until Tate gave a nod. "We'll find him later. Right at the moment, I can see that you are exhausted and hungry. Come into the house with me. We'll get you cleaned up and some food into you. And I suspect that you could use a soft bed to sleep in for a while."

Tate blinked. This was not what she had expected. Sudden tears blinded her. She couldn't look up, couldn't rise.

Mae gave a soft sound and then her arm was around Tate as she prayed for her. Tate leaned against her, feeling the love of a mother for the first time in years. Rising, Mae tugged Tate to her feet and into the house.

"Here, I'm Mae. Don't worry about danger. I'm a retired officer and still work in the auxiliary portion. I have good security here as well. Now, we'll get you cleaned up. I have some clothes that a niece forgot here. They should fit you. Just some leggings and T-shirts. There is some lingerie as well that has never come out of the package. She would tell you to use it." Mae was chattering away, not like her at all, her arm still around Tate as she led her to a spare room. "In here. Take your time, Tate. I'll find us some food. It will soon be lunchtime. Then you'll sleep and then we'll talk."

Tate nodded at last, turning slightly as the door closed softly behind Mae. This was not what she had expected. Not at all. She reached for the clothes that Mae had set on the bed, a sigh drawn from her. She had only been renting a room, using her landlady's phone if she needed to. She had nothing of value, other than her Bible, and she knew that her landlady would simply pack her things and keep them for her. Her work at a fast-food restaurant was only enough to barely survive. She couldn't find anything better, no matter how she had tried.

Showered, her hair washed, Tate felt refreshed. She paused for a moment before she sat on the double bed, feeling the softness of the blankets. Tate's eye closed for a moment as she prayed. Prayer had become an important part of her life in the last few years, she knew. God was with her, she believed. She just didn't understand why she had been abducted or what the men wanted from her.

Mae turned as she heard Tate's soft footsteps approaching her, stopping at the kitchen table.

"Feel better? I know I always do when I get cleaned up." Mae reached to hug her once more, Tate returning the hug. "We'll talk, Tate. But first, let's get some food into you. A friend is coming by to join us."

Tate looked up in fear, her mouth opening and closing. It wasn't her house so she couldn't refuse.

"It's okay. It's Bill. He drops by every once in a while. I was his supervisor when he first joined the county force. He has become a good friend over the years. He doesn't know that you are here. We'll keep that very low key until we talk with him." Mae finally made Tate sit, setting a mug of tea in front of her. "You drink tea?"

Tate nodded, finally relaxing. She felt safe with Mae and then hopeful for a change.

"I do. I've made you a lot of work." Tate blinked against sudden tears, ashamed of them and then ashamed that she wasn't strong enough not to cry.

"No, not really. Now that we know where you are, we'll do our best to keep you safe. We've been looking for you." Mae looked up as she heard a tap at the door and then footsteps heading their way. "Welcome, Bill."

Bill stopped abruptly, shock briefly on his face. How did Tate come to be here?

"Mae?"

"It's okay, Bill." She stood with an arm around Tate's shoulders. "Tate showed up here today and is now my guest. We'll eat and then we'll talk. I think Tate has a tale to tell us that we need to hear. And then we'll find Timothy and reunite them. I know how worried he has been."

Bill nodded, jacket hitting the back of a chair before he reached for the coffee carafe, filling his mug. Mae didn't drink coffee herself but kept it on hand for her friends.

Bill ate his lunch, quiet conversation between himself and Mae. He watched Tate closely, seeing how on edge she was. No, he corrected himself, how close to the edge she was. It wouldn't take much to shove her all the way over. That he wanted to avoid.

"How did you find Tate, Mae?" Bill was on his feet, helping to clear away the debris from their lunch before he was refilling the ladies' tea cups and his own mug of coffee. He was back in his chair, his laptop open. He had questioned Mae when she told him that he needed it. Now he understood.

"She was on my front steps. Just sitting there watching Timothy's house. It wasn't too long after he came home. I approached her, got her into the house, and cleaned up."

"I see." Bill turned to Tate, finding her watching him, a cautious look on her face and fear in her eyes. She didn't trust them, he thought. "Okay, then. Tate, let's talk. Tell me exactly what happened to you, where you're from, and where you've been for the last week."

Tate searched Mae's face, seeing her nodding at her, a smile on her face. Then, she turned to Bill, searching his face. She finally nodded.

"Okay. I'm just not sure where to start. I'm not from here. I am actually from another province. I moved here when I was eighteen. My parents didn't want me and I didn't want to stay near them."

Bill and Mae shared a look. This was not what they had expected to hear.

Chapter 7

Tate rubbed at her thighs, her eyes searching for answers. She liked the comfortable feeling of Mae's kitchen, the soft autumn colours that she had used. She even liked the retro chrome table and chairs that Mae had recovered and used on a daily basis.

"I don't know where to start." Tate was at a loss to know that.

"How about your early life?" Bill had his notebook out, knowing that he would need it.

Tate shrugged, knowing that she had to but also knowing that it would bring up memories that she had buried and had no intention of ever revisiting.

"It's hard, isn't it, Tate?" Mae's arm was around her again and her prayer whispered in the young lady's ear. "God is here and He understands. He has allowed this for His own reasons. We will work with you on this. We will never ever walk away from you."

Tate had turned her face to watch Mae as she spoke. She nodded.

"I get that, Mae. I have never had that before. I have moved from town to town, working odd jobs, low paying jobs, just earring enough to rent a room. I have no memories with me. The only thing that I want from my last place is my Bible. The landlady will hold onto it for me."

"What town was that?" Bill's pen was posed over the notepad.

"Holly. I was there for about six months until this happened. I don't know who did this. I really don't."

"That's not too far from here." Bill watched her closely. "You rented a room there?"

"I did. I worked in a sandwich shop part time. There was only enough money really for rent and one meal a day. It was hard."

"I understand." Bill looked down for a moment. "Tell me about your parents. What did they do? Why would they want you to leave?"

"You know, I'm not sure exactly what they did. Business of some kind. They never really said. And I just never asked. I guess I was told too many times that it wasn't my business and I just stopped asking. I should have kept on, I guess. Any way, when I was eighteen, they told me to leave. That they had never wanted me and wanted nothing more to do with me. That hurt, even though they had been distant all my life. I was done school and had just obtained a summer job. I left, found a room, and worked. They made it difficult for me to stay in my hometown. So I left. I moved across the country over the past years, working until I had enough saved so that I could catch a bus. I am from Saskatchewan. I have no idea why I chose Ontario and Southern Ontario at that. I guess that you could say God led me here. I didn't have many friends at home. I was shunned, I realize now. I have no idea why that would be. It has to come back to my parents." She looked up at that point, a hurt look deep in her eyes.

Bill nodded, knowing that she was saying just how her life had been. He had heard it many times before in many different ways

"I'll get your parents' name in a bit and then we'll look into that." He reached for the paper that Tate was sliding towards him. "These are their names? Thank you, Tate. You're ahead of me."

"Mae suggested it. She thought that you would want that." Tate grew silent for a moment. "And I want to know why. It's hung over me all my life. I don't know who the other relatives are. They never talked about their family. Do I have aunts, uncles, cousins, grandparents out there who want me?"

"We'll look into it for you. That's a promise." Bill looked down at his notes. "Now, as to what happened last week. Can you tell me?" He looked up as she remained silent. "It's important that we know, Tate. It involves Timothy now as well. His family and team members are concerned about that. He can't explain it."

Tate nodded, reaching to sip from her cup of tea, not realizing that it was now cold. It wouldn't have mattered if she had realized that. She just needed something to do for a moment while she composed her thoughts.

"I really don't know what happened. That Friday night, my landlady knocked at my door and told me that someone wanted to speak with me. They were waiting outside for me. I went down and outside. It was dusk, so I couldn't see very well. I walked out onto the sidewalk and then someone had simply clapped a hand over my mouth and bundled me into a car. I didn't get a chance to scream or even try to escape. We drove around for a while. I couldn't speak at all. I was terrified. They made sure that I knew they would kill me if I spoke or tried to escape. They brought me here in the early morning and to that area. I was made to stand there. I was afraid to look around, to see if someone would help me. I could hear conversation around me but I just couldn't respond.

"When Timothy approached, they stopped him. They wouldn't let him pass them. Then they started to beat him. I was too afraid to move. One of the men was standing behind me, threatening anyone around me. They left at last. Timothy made it to his feet and then to me. I don't know him. I didn't know what he wanted. He seemed to sense that I was afraid. He took my hand and started away. That's when he collapsed." Tate looked up at that point. Mae and Bill could see the fear and also the lack of understanding on her face. "What did I do, Bill?"

"I don't think that you have done anything, Tate. At least, not that I can see for now. Even if it does come back to something in your past, it isn't your fault. It never is." Bill studied his notes. "I have your statement and can print it off for you to read through and sign. If there are any more questions, then we can and will talk. Sometimes things are remembered after the fact. Keep a diary of that and let me know."

"How do I keep Timothy away from me?" Tate had not heard the door open and new footsteps heading her way.

—

Timothy stood for a moment, in shock as he stared at Tate. Mae was on her feet, drawing him into the living room, praying for her young friend.

"Mae? Where did Tate come from?" Timothy turned to face the kitchen, hearing the quiet conversation between Bill and Tate.

"She followed you this morning, Timothy. I found her sitting on the front steps. She'll stay with me for now." Mae watched with compassion as Timothy worked to control his emotions.

"Your front steps? I didn't see her."

"She didn't want you to. She is unsure if she should stay here. I would like her to, but we have to let her make that decision. You also need to get her to speak with you. She has a rough history and that will impact her trust issues. Just let her know that you are there for her and are praying for her."

"I can do that." Timothy sighed, a hand rubbing at his cheek. "I have no idea what we're mixed up in."

"None of us do at this time." Mae nodded towards the kitchen. "How you react right now with her, how you speak with her will determine where you go with her. You know that from your work."

"I do, unfortunately. Only God can give me the words that I need." Timothy prayed for a moment before his feet took him towards the lady who he had spent the last week searching for.

Chapter 8

Timothy waited in the doorway, his eyes on Tate. Bill had looked up briefly before he looked back at Tate. Tate sat quietly, reading through her statement, a hand propping up her head. Both men could see the fatigue in her, fatigue that went back many years and not from the past week. It was more than just physical fatigue.

Tate slid the paperwork across the table to Bill, a sigh rising from deep within her. Her past was out there now, not where she wanted it to be but in a way, she was glad that it was. Her eyes rose as she heard a slight sound. Timothy had moved towards her, a chair pulled back to that he could sit next to her. He took the mug of coffee that Mae extend to him.

"Tate? Are you okay?" Timothy had been deeply worried about her.

"No, I don't think that I am, Timothy. I don't know that I have ever been." Tate's eyes grew heavy. "I'm sorry. I need to sleep." She was on her feet, moving quickly away from them. She headed for the room that she had been told to use. She was asleep almost before she had laid down, not even bothering to cover herself.

Mae had followed her, worry for her young friend on her face. She reached for a quilt, tucking it around Tate, a hand resting lightly on her hair as she prayed for her.

Timothy stood in the kitchen doorway, listening to Bill on the phone behind him. His eyes didn't move from the room where Tate had taken refuge. He wanted to go to her but he couldn't. He might never be able to.

Mae approached him, reaching to hug him, and then past him towards where Bill was tucking away his phone.

"Bill? What now? What do we do for her?" Mae reached to tidy away their mugs, an eye on the clock. It wasn't near suppertime but she didn't think any of them would feel much like eating.

"I do some investigating. I didn't like what I heard but that's par for the course in cases like this." He was frustrated.

"I know it is. I can reach out to someone I know in her town. A friend who is on the force."

"You have a friend out there?" Bill was surprised. "God was at work there, wasn't He?" He grinned at her for a moment. "Do that. Let me have your friend's name as well. I'll reach out on an official basis. Tate's hurting, Mae. I don't know how we can reach her."

"Gently, Bill. By being her friend. By making her feel safe." Mae watched as Timothy stood near her. "If we have to, we have to let her go. She's not a prisoner. We can't make her stay if she doesn't want to."

"No, we can't. Not unless we put her into protective custody." Bill hesitated for a moment, not

---

sure what else to say. "Stay as close as she'll let you. Timothy, you're back at work on Monday. Don't stop that because of Tate. She'll resent that."

"I know, Bill. I can't stop work, as much as I would like to." Timothy reached for his phone. It had been vibrating incessantly. "I'm sorry. I need to take this call." He walked away, to find a seat on Mae's front porch. "Richard?"

"Timothy? Where are you?" Richard's voice was rushed.

"At Mae's. Why?" Timothy could hear the traffic in the background of the call.

"Stay put. We're on our way there." Richard's voice cut off as he dropped the call.

Timothy stared at his phone and then shrugged, tucking his phone away. He nodded at Bill as the other man moved away, content for the moment to sit on the porch and wait.

Mae sat near him, her eyes closing as she prayed for her friends. She could feel the storm gathering around her young friends.

Richard walked towards the house, Silver beside him. Naomi and Stephen headed around the house before heading for Timothy's. Timothy and Mae watched, having a good idea what was happening.

"What did they threaten, Richard?" Timothy was resigned.

"You. Somehow they have figured out where Tate is. And that brings danger to Mae as well."

—

"I know that, Richard. Do you really think I care?" Mae was matter-of-fact in her statement. The sounds of nature echoed in their ears as a faint breeze blew around them.

"We know that you don't, Mae, and that you are more than capable of defending yourself. It's just that we don't know who or why." Richard perched on the porch railing, a position he had assumed many times in the past.

"No, we don't. We know some more about Tate. She told us that her family basically kicked her out when she was eighteen, told her that she had never been wanted. She's been moving across the country for years."

"That's sad." Silver turned for a moment before she was across the street, moving towards Naomi.

Richard had turned, watching the trio, before he turned back to Timothy.

"You locked up, Timothy?"

Timothy nodded, on his feet, heading for the stairs.

"I did. This must mean that they found something." He was away before Richard could respond.

"How much danger is he in, Richard?" Mae finally spoke.

"We don't know, Mae. We really don't know. We're getting rumours from the streets but nothing concrete."

"That's about where you would stand at this point. We need to do some research, don't we?" Mae lived for that kind of work.

"We do. If you can work on that, we'd appreciate it." Richard drew his upper lip down over his teeth. "From your point of view, Mae, how is Tate?"

"Tate?" She turned her head for a moment to look towards the front door. "She's hurting, Richard, as I said. She is confused. She has no idea who the men were or why they took her. She's worked minimum wage jobs since she was eighteen. She hasn't been to college. She has only had enough to rent a room and for food. She didn't say but I would suggest that she has gone hungry on more than one occasion."

Richard drew a deep breath. It was about what he had expected to hear. Only he had prayed that he wouldn't.

"What do we do then, Mae? How do we help her? Do we need to go and retrieve whatever it is that she left behind?"

"She has clothing and her Bible at her last place. She said her landlady would keep them for her."

"We'll get them. I'll talk to one of the guys and see which ones we can free up to send that way. I know our friends would do that."

"They will. Talk to Gareth or Tag. Tag and his friends would be the ones to go, if they're available. They'd know the questions to ask."

Chapter 9

Timothy stood in his backyard, watching as Bill and the crime scene techs moved through it. He didn't like that feeling he had, that his sanctuary had been invaded. And it had been in the worst possible way. The bomb squad had been there and removed the package, warning Timothy to be extremely careful. He had no idea who had placed it but he suspected that it was related to Tate. That lady had not yet appeared. Mae had sent Richard to him, simply stating that Tate was still sleeping.

Walking through his house, Timothy searched for any evidence that someone had been there. He didn't see anything but he knew that they had likely made a try. He had a security system that was one of the best and a strong password that no one should be able to guess.

Richard stood for a moment, watching Timothy. This shouldn't be happening, he knew. Unfortunately, just because Timothy had stepped in to help a lady in trouble, he had become a target of someone. They just didn't know who or why.

"Richard? Any word?" Timothy stopped near him, turning to study his living room. His hands were jammed into the pocket of his sweatshirt.

"Not yet. Bill said he'd be in shortly to speak with you. I don't like it, Timothy." Richard was worried and for Richard to be worried meant that he acted. "I have no idea what to do for you."

"I know, Richard. Neither do I. It's just so strange. I still don't remember being attacked. I heard what Tate told Bill. I just can't recall anything about the men." Timothy was frustrated and it showed.

Silver, Naomi, and Stephen were around, Timothy knew, watching his house and watching Mae's house. Mae was still on her porch, waiting for Timothy to return. She knew that he would, that he would want to be near where Tate was.

Tate paused in the doorway before she came out to sit where Timothy had sat. She was still only half awake and yawned.

Mae grinned at her.

"Did you have a good sleep, Tate?"

Tate nodded, her eyes catching the activity across the street.

"I did. What's going on over there?"

"I have no idea. Timothy and Richard will be back shortly, I think. There has been a lot of activity, I know." Mae reached for Tate's hand, praying audibly for her friend. "You are not alone, Tate. Never again. You have friends here who will help you get through whatever this is. And you know that Timothy is not going to walk away from you. It's not in him to do that."

"That's what I'm afraid of, Mae. That he won't and that he'll be hurt worse than he was. I don't want that on my conscious." Tate took her hand back and wrapped her arms around herself. She knew that she needed to disappear again and move to another town.

Only, this time around she didn't want to. She liked Elmton and the people who she had met, even the ones on the street.

Timothy walked back towards Mae, a slump to his shoulders. He had sent his friends home, simply stating that there wasn't anything else that they could do. Knowing that they had plans for that night, he just wouldn't let them stay any longer. Richard had watched him walk away, worried about him but confident that God was in control. He just feared for what his friend might be facing.

Timothy slumped into a chair, his chin dropping. He was exhausted, he decided, and should have stayed at home. But the lady sitting near him drew him to Mae's.

"Timothy?" Mae's voice broke into his thoughts. "What was that all about?"

Timothy looked around, not surprised to see Tate there. He studied her and then Mae's property, taking in the shrubs, bushes, and plants that she tended regularly. He loved her gardens.

"A bomb, Mae. Someone set a bomb in my backyard."

"A bomb?" Tate stared at him. "Did you just say a bomb?" She was horrified at the thought.

"I did. I don't know who or why, Tate. We don't know that it is related to you. We don't have enough information to confirm that." Timothy's head dropped once more. The headache that he had started fighting hours ago had worsened and it was making it difficult for him to concentrate and think straight. "It could be related to my work."

"And just what do you do? I have never been told." Tate was frustrated and it came out in her words

"I work on a security team. Richard is my boss. Silver, Stephen, and Naomi are my team mates." He squinted as he watched her reaction.

"A security team?" Tate sat back in the wicker chair, her hands on her cheeks. "As is keeping someone safe? And just how do they keep you safe if you're one of the team?"

"That's something we will work on. We have friends on another security team who all went through danger with their ladies." Timothy grinned at Mae as she snorted.

"Their ladies?" Tate was dumbstruck for a moment. "There is no way that I am your lady. No way."

"We know that, Tate. Just think about this. At some point, we may need to portray that we are. That would be to keep you safe. Until we understand better why you were kidnapped like you were and then brought here, we don't know who is behind that. And we want to solve it very quickly, or as quickly as we can." Timothy's eyes closed for a moment. He heard soft rustling as someone rose. He cracked open one eye to see that Tate had left.

"She needs time, Timothy, to absorb what you have said and to come to some sort of understanding. She has been on her own for so long, feeling unwanted, that she is not certain who she can trust or who will hurt her." Mae had a sad look on her face. "We don't know what that is like, unfortunately. Both of us have families that love us or loved us and who we love in return. She has never felt as if she has had that."

Timothy nodded, sadness covering his face.

"It's so sad, Mae. How do we make sure that she understands that?"

"It's not something that we can force on her, Timothy. It's like when your team is out. Some of those who you protect don't trust you or it takes time for them to trust you. All we can do is pray for her. God will work in her life and heart. He will be the One who will guide her in this. All we can do is be there for her, support her in her decisions no matter if we think that they are not the ones that she should be making, and pray for her. I have asked her to stay with me for now. She was not certain that she should but she has agreed to. I just don't know how long that will be."

Timothy's eyes raised to look behind Mae, seeing Tate standing her, a little girl lost look on her face. He was on his feet, reaching to draw her into a hug. He felt the tears when they started and could only hold her as she wept.

Chapter 10

Tate sat quietly the next morning, her eyes on the front of the church. It was not like any church where she had ever been. Not that she had been able to attend church much with her working most Sundays. She had felt that intensely when it first happened and then she had just gotten used to it.

Timothy sat on one side of her, Mae on her other. They had shared looks over her head before Timothy had turned as he felt a hand on his shoulder. Stephen sat beside him, Silver and Naomi next to him.

"Timothy? How are you?" Stephen's voice was low, the concern that he was feeling showing in his eyes.

Timothy shrugged.

"I'm getting there. I just needed to be here today, Stephen." He nodded towards Tate. "She needs our support."

"She does and she has it." Silver leaned forward to study the other lady. "She's sad, Timothy."

"She is, Silver." Timothy had kept his voice low, hoping that Tate had not heard him. He could hear Mae's voice speaking with Tate and he breathed a sigh of relief. Mae had picked up on that for him and he was grateful.

Stephen nodded, his attention going back to the front as the worship team started up. He would talk with Timothy later. But later never came. Richard came to find the three before the service was over, shaking his head at Timothy. Timothy watched them walk away, jumping as he felt a hand on his. Tate had been watching him at that point and reached out to him.

Once the service was over, Tate watched him closer.

"Are you okay, Timothy?"

Timothy shrugged, not sure how to respond. He wanted to be with his friends and team mates but knew that he couldn't be. He had not been cleared to return to that work as yet.

"I don't know, Tate. So, how was the service?" He grinned at her as she stared at him. She had not expected the change of topic.

"It was interesting, to say the least. The pastor is good." She stared harder at him as he continued to laugh. "What's so funny about that?"

"I need to introduce you to Silas and Madison. They had an adventure that you need to hear about." He was on his feet, reaching for her hand, nodding as Mae pointed towards the front of the church. "Mae will be a while. Did you want to wait for her or come with me?"

Tate chewed at her lip, not sure what to do. She watched closely as Timothy was greeted and then introduced to the people in the church. She lost track of who they all were.

Timothy took pity on her and drew her away and to the outside. He found Richard waiting for him.

"Richard? What's going on?"

"Where are you heading, Timothy?" Richard's eyes were in constant motion.

"I'm not sure. Likely home? Why?" Timothy's hand tightened on Tate's as she tried to pull away from him.

"Okay. Did you drive or did Mae?"

"I drove myself. Tate came with Mae but I'm taking her with me." Timothy walked towards his car, finding Stephen, Silver, and Naomi there. "Richard? What is going on"

"Bill called me. Someone has called in a threat against you. We have no idea as yet who or why. And they mentioned Tate." Richard paused beside Timothy's car. "For now, your car stays here. Bill has a team coming out to go over it."

Timothy's face paled as he took in the implications of what Richard had said. He pulled Tate with him as Richard pointed towards his own truck.

Tate dug in her heels, not wanting to be pulled all over the parking lot, she decided.

"Timothy? Why not your car?"

"Because it may have been tampered and we can't take a chance on that." Timothy yanked open the truck door and shoved Tate inside, sitting beside her and shutting the door. "Now, stop. We are both at risk and Richard is trying to come up with a plan and place to keep us safe. It's what we do, Tate."

Tate finally nodded, her eyes on Richard as he slid behind the wheel, his phone out as he spoke to someone. He pocketed his phone and just sat there, his

—

fingers tapping on the steering wheel. Bill had called, asking that he wait for him to appear

"Richard?"   Timothy's voice finally broke through the silence.

"Timothy? Tate? Bill is on his way. He wants to speak with both of you. That may mean putting you two away somewhere."

"And you have that group to work with this week." Timothy was running through the work that he knew was on the books.

"It's not a problem, Timothy. Abe and Don have both offered to step in."

"I thought that they would. It doesn't make it any easier."   Timothy's hand reached for Tate's, finding hers cold under his touch. "Tate, Abe and Don are friends. They also have security teams and will step in if we need them to."

"Okay. So where are we heading now? I want to go back to Mae's."   Tate had felt safe there and didn't want to go anywhere that would destroy that.

"We'll head for Mae's, Tate. For now, it's okay. Timothy's home is secure as well. You two should be safe. We won't keep you together at this point, unless we need to." Richard was out of the truck and walking towards Bill. They stood deep in talk for a while.

Timothy watched as the crime scene techs searched around his car, taking his keys from him at one point. Tate watched Timothy, a frown on her face. She didn't understand why he still held her hand or why he was just sitting there, not out there in the midst of what was going on.

"Timothy? Shouldn't you be out there?" Tate finally voiced her question.

Timothy shook his head, turning to face her.

"No, I'm where I need to be. With you. One, to try and keep you as safe as I can. Secondly, because I am a victim of this as well. Richard wants to keep us together and not have two places to protect."

Tate stared at him harder, her eyes then moving to watch Richard through the window. Stephen and Naomi had approached the truck, one of each side, their backs to the vehicle. Silver was near Timothy's vehicle, her gaze not on what was happening there but on the crowd that had gathered.

"What happens now, then? Can't we go back to Mae's?" Tate was tired, just wanting to crawl into bed and sleep.

"We wait for a while. And we will go back to Mae's. At least that is the plan. If it changes, Richard and Bill will have discussed that and made the decision of where best to place us."

"Is Mae in danger?" Tate was worried about her. Mae had taken on the role of a mother to Tate, something that Tate didn't know that she had ever had.

"She may be, but she's aware of the danger and what she needs to do. We would have no hesitation of leaving you in her care." Timothy reached to tuck a curl behind Tate's ear. "We will do our very best to keep you safe. That's a promise to you. God will give us the information we need to do that.

"And what if your best is not enough? What happens then?"

Chapter 11

Bill stared at Timothy's car. It had been cleared, with nothing found. Richard was beside him, Andrew on Bill's other side.

"Bill? What's the word?" Richard spoke at last, shifting his stance to watch his truck as well. His four team members stood there and he could see Tate watching them all from inside his truck.

"It's clear. It's strange, what the call was about. Who is this person after? Timothy or Tate?" Bill was genuinely puzzled.

"I would suspect both of them." Andrew walked around Timothy's car, a frown on his face. "Any further information on whoever it was?"

Bill shook his head, puzzled as well.

"I have no more information on that. Jason's working on that and even he has reached a roadblock. That's not what happens in our town."

"No, it's not." Richard turned as he heard his name called and excused himself to walk away. "Don? I thought that you were out of town."

"No, we finished early. Bad situation all around. What's this I have heard?" Don reached to shake Richard's hand.

"If you heard that Timothy is in danger, then it's true." Richard drew in a deep breath. Don was a lifelong friend, the two men growing up in side by side houses. "And then there's Tate."

"Tate? I met a lady with that name but not from here. It's been a couple of years." Don turned carefully, searching the diminishing crowd. "Someone is out here, Richard, someone we know well."

"I know. We can all feel whoever it is." Richard pointed towards his truck. "That's her in my truck."

Don studied her and then nodded.

"That's her. We need to talk, Don. Your team and my team. But my team is tied up with that group in town this week. Timothy's not working, not given the injuries that he suffered a week ago. He's not cleared yet to go back to his full duties."

"And you're short a man. Let me talk with my guys. We're in the office this week, doing paperwork and training. One of my guys can be freed up to work with you every day. And I can likely put someone with both Timothy and Tate." Don walked away at that, his mind working as to who he could free up. He knew without asking that his guys would do that. It's what he and Richard did. And he knew that Abe would do the same. His phone was out as he called Abe, simply leaving a message for Abe to call either himself or Richard.

Timothy shifted from foot to foot. He was uncomfortable, just standing there. He wanted to get Tate home and safe. Only he had no idea where that would be. Mae had been around, speaking quietly with the two before she headed home.

Tate watched the activity, growing tired of just sitting. When would they be able to leave? She refused to ask, catching Andrew's eye for a moment.

—

No, she thought, *I can't do this. I need to leave. Only I don't think that Timothy will let me. And Lord, end this please soon? This is not good for any of us. And I don't want anyone hurt.*

Andrew walked towards Richard and Bill, his wife, Phoebe, with him. Phoebe stopped for a moment and then headed towards Timothy and Tate.

"Timothy? Are you okay?" She reached to hug him before she stood, patiently waiting for him to speak.

Timothy shrugged, not sure what to say. He didn't think that he was okay, but he wasn't sure on that. He stared up to the bright blue sky, watching for the storm clouds that were gathering. Only they weren't visible.

"Introduce me to your friend, Timothy." Phoebe moved towards the truck, a hand out to shake Tate's. "Hello, I'm Phoebe McBeth. Andrew is my husband. I think that you have met him."

Tate hesitated before she nodded.

"I think I have. Right at the moment, I don't know who I have or haven't met."

Phoebe laughed at that.

"So, are you heading for your home? If I could come with you, I would like that." Phoebe had no hesitation about inviting herself to go with Tate.

Tate stared at her, not sure how to respond. She could hear the laughter from Timothy and his team.

"No, I'm not. I don't have a home here. I'm staying with Mae. But I think that I need to leave town." Tate was adamant on that.

"We can't have you doing that, Tate." Phoebe was just as adamant on that. "Listen, Timothy. Have they said how long your car will be?"

Timothy shook his head.

"No, they haven't but I suspect it will be a while. I need to get Tate out of here."

"Come on then, Tate. Let's head out." Phoebe had the truck door open and Tate out of it an walking towards her car. "Andrew's parents have our little one today, so I'm free to go with you. Timothy, are you coming?"

Timothy shook his head, a slight smile on his face as he saw the look on Tate's face. She's not sure what to do and that could get her hurt.

Silver laughed as she and Naomi followed the two ladies, chatter between them. Timothy simply watched them walk away before his eyes raised to the small group that still remained. He sighed to himself. This is not how he planned today. He had wanted to take both Tate and Mae out for lunch. That was not happening, he knew.

Stephen watched his friend closely. He knew that Timothy was deeply troubled and worried. He turned as he heard footsteps, frowning at the man who had appeared.

"Abe? What are you doing here?"

Abe Finlay grinned for a moment before he sobered.

"Emma sent me. She's concerned about Timothy. She just didn't know why." Abe had a security team that was devoted now to mostly training other teams. His wife, Emma, had an investigative firm called Trackers. She was able to find people and information that no one else seemed able to.

Timothy had turned as he heard Abe's voice. He nodded. Emma was weighing in and that would help.

Chapter 12

"Abe?" Timothy stared at his friend, not quite sure what was happening. "What did Emma do?"

Abe began to laugh.

"Not Emma, this time. It was Jace and Naomi." He held up a folder. "We'll need to go over this at some point today." Abe frowned, sharing a look with Stephen, who simply shook his head.

"Jace?" Timothy paced away from the two men, heading for Andrew. "Andrew? What have you come up with?"

Andrew turned as he heard Timothy.

"I'm not sure what all we've found, Timothy. We're towing your car, that's a given. And someone will drive you home. Now, where's Tate?"

"Tate? She left with Phoebe, Silver, and Naomi. I think they were heading for Mae's." Timothy turned and paced between his two groups of friends. He wasn't sure where he wanted to be, other than with Tate and that wasn't happening at the moment. He paused for a moment, catching sight of someone watching him. A frown on his face, he walked towards the man.

"David? What are you doing here?"

"Looking for you." David Long, a long-time friend of Timothy's, studied his friend and then the activity in the church parking lot.

"You are? Why?" Timothy stood beside him, his back to the activity.

"I heard what happened to you. I was worried." David watched his friend closely. "I might have information for you. Where can we talk?"

"At my place?" Timothy rubbed at his face. "No, that won't work. I want Tate in on our conversation. It involves her."

"It does, Timothy. Where is she?" David had just arrived and missed the ladies leaving.

"At Mae's. That would work, going there. Mae would be fine with that, I know." Timothy turned as he heard footsteps approaching and when he turned back, David had disappeared.

Bill stood near him, a frown on his face.

"Who was that, Timothy?"

"A friend. David Long. We're meeting today. He seems to think he has information for me. At least, I think that's what he implied."

Bill nodded.

"It will be a while before we tow your car. We're taking it to the police garage to go over it better. Let's get you home." Bill knew that Richard and Stephen were waiting nearby.

Timothy sighed, sudden fatigue hitting him. He had not been sleeping well, determined to stay awake and watch Mae's home. He had such a burden for Tate. He just couldn't figure out how he had become involved in her life.

———

"Yeah, I guess." Timothy's steps were slow and heavy as he walked towards his friends.

Stephen and Richard shared a look. This was different, they knew, trying to protect a friend and team mate rather than strangers.

"Ready to go, Timothy? Stephen's driving." Richard watched as the two men walked away before he turned to Bill. "Who was that with Timothy?"

"Someone named David Long. A friend, he said." Bill waited for Richard to react, his eyes studying the people remaining. All were from the church or were law enforcement but he still felt the presence of evil surrounding them.

"David? He's been around lately. He had moved from here, Timothy said, and then moved back about six months ago. He's a builder, doing historical renovations. Timothy didn't know how long he would be around here. There's something in his past that Timothy isn't saying."

"Just what we need, Richard. Another angle to this case. We're at a loss to know why. Timothy doesn't have any enemies that we know about. Tate? Now, there's a lady who isn't talking much. I don't know if she has any enemies."

"No, she doesn't say much. A lot goes back to being on her own for so many years. She has learned to keep her life private. And it likely goes back to how she was removed from her home. What teenage girl wants to be told she's not wanted by her parents."

Bill nodded.

—

"That's what I don't understand." He looked down at the keys that he held in his hand. "I need to run. Cora and Michael are waiting for me. We had plans that we've had to delay. I hate to do that."

"Go on, Bill. Jason's on duty, isn't he? Send him around to Mae's." Richard walked away, intent on heading for Mae's. His steps slowed as he approached his truck before he reached for the envelope tucked under his windshield wiper. He sighed. What next? He turned to look for either Bill or Jason but neither was there.

Opening the envelope, Richard stared down at the photo. It was of Timothy from the day before, standing on his back deck, a mug in his hand. Tate was sitting nearby as was Mae. Richard grew angry for a moment and then sighed. *Lord, I don't understand, but You do. You have our friends in Your hands. This is far from over, we know, but please protect our friends, heal them, and bring whatever this is to a quick resolution. And don't let the rest of us face anything like this. I am afraid for my team.*

Richard slipped behind the wheel of his truck, the envelope sitting on the passenger's seat. He studied it once more and then headed for the police department. This needed to go to Bill and he had no idea where Bill was at that moment. Bill was off with his family and he would not disturb him.

Jason Long turned as he heard his name called, pausing as he walked towards the police department building.

"Richard? What are you doing here? I thought that you would be with Timothy?" Jason was a friend of them all and also a detective.

"I was heading that way. I found this on my truck." He handed over the envelope. "A photo of Timothy, Tate, and Mae. Taken yesterday. I have no idea who left it but I only saw your people and the people from the church around."

Jason's hand paused as he reached for the envelope.

"Are you saying someone from the church? That they're involved?"

"I would say so, but I'm not certain. I'll work on a list of names of the people who were there. Our team's hurting, Jason."

"I get that, Richard. Get us the list when you can. I had to think that it would be someone from there but that's happened before. Look at Silas and Madigan."

"I know. That's what I was thinking." Richard walked away, leaving Jason staring at the envelope before he too sighed and headed inside.

Chapter 13

Timothy took the plate of food handed to him and turned, searching for Tate. He wanted to be near her. In fact, he was driven to be there. Tate wasn't hungry but knew that she had to eat. Her appetite was just not there. She watched as Timothy headed her way, two plates in his hands.

"Tate? Here. Mae fixed this for you." Timothy sat on the couch beside her, listening to the chatter and laughter around him. "It's okay. We know that you're not hungry but could you eat something?"

"I can." Tate blinked to clear the tears from her eyes. Timothy's compassion and caring for her were not what she had expected. He didn't smother her but made sure that she was taken care of.

Tate nibbled at her meal, her eyes searching the faces of each one seated around the room. The ladies had become dear to her but she was afraid for them. She had heard their stories and knew that Silver and Naomi were on guard, not wanting her to be harmed. They could see the interest in Tate that Timothy was trying hard to hide.

"Are you okay?" Timothy reached for Tate's plate and set it aside on top of his.

Tate shrugged.

"I'm not sure, Timothy. I'm not sure how I'm to feel." She turned to him, her eyes searching his. "And how are you? This has disrupted your life. I'm sorry."

"We don't know which one of us is the target. Not yet. Today? That was a warning sent to us. Bill and Jason are working on it." Timothy's eyes lifted as he saw Richard approaching them and sitting nearby. "Richard? What else happened?"

"I found a photo of you three on my truck when I went to leave the church. It's disturbing, Timothy, Tate. We are praying for your protection but not knowing who it is has us very concerned and worried."

"I know that, Richard. God is in control, we all agree on that. But how do we find this person before one of us is killed?" Tate was not backing down from them, not any more. She had decided that wasn't working out so well.

"We all agree on that, Tate. As to where we go? That may mean you two making a list of everyone that you can think of. Tate, we need to know who your family is. We need their names, relationship to you, that kind of stuff." He grinned as she glared at him. "It's what Bill will be asking you shortly. He needs that kind of information."

"I know that, Richard. I get that we need to look at them. I just don't have to like it." She looked down, blinking rapidly at the tears that gathered, tears that she couldn't control.

Timothy gave a sound and then just swept her into a hug. He felt her jump and then relax against him. He took the handkerchief handed to him with a word of thanks.

Richard watched with compassion as Tate struggled with her emotions. She was going through a

—

lot right now, he knew. He could see her fighting her feelings already for Timothy, not sure if she should have any other than gratitude. Richard has seen it too many times but this time it was different. This was his friend who was involved.

Timothy was watching the interaction between the two, an amused look lurking in his eyes. He was curious to see who would win. His thought was that it would be Tate. Instead, Tate nodded, a deep sigh drawn from her.

"You think it's someone from my past or someone I've met? But that doesn't explain Timothy's involvement. I have never met any of you. In fact, I wasn't living here. I was living in Holly." She closed her eyes for a moment. "I need to go back and grab my stuff."

"And we'll get you there this week. We're around mid-week." Richard rose, staring down at the floor for a moment. "Never forget, Tate, that God loves you. He has you in His hands. He knew before time began that you would face this. He has a plan in place for you and that plan is for your good. It's hard to trust when the storm clouds are surrounding you. He is there. Just remember that He calms the storms, sometimes around us, sometimes within us." Richard walked away, leaving Tate staring after him.

"Richard's correct, Tate. God really does that."

"I know, Timothy. It's hard to understand that God cares and loves for us like He does." Tate settled back against him, not realizing that he still had his arms around her.

—

72

Mae approached, a smile on her face that she quickly covered. Yes, she thought, they are interested in one another. She sat nearby, her mug of tea in her hands.

"Tate? When were you thinking of going back to Holly?"

"Richard thinks mid-week. I don't want to go back there but I have to."

Timothy shared a look with Mae. There was a reason that she didn't want to. He just wasn't sure if she would tell him.

Silver had been listening and decided to get involved.

"Why don't you want to go back, Tate? Did something happen?"

Tate shook her head, a frown on her face.

"Not that I know of. I just never felt safe." She snorted, causing Timothy to grin for a moment. "I haven't felt safe for years. Not like you all have. You've had your family to be with, your friends. I've been on my own. I don't have close friends. My family disowned me." Tate drew in a shuddering breath, her eyes on the painting above the fireplace. "It hasn't been easy."

"We understand that it hasn't been, Tate." Mae moved to sit beside her. "Now, if you were to write down your feelings and thoughts. Sometimes that makes it easier."

Tate had turned to Mae, a nod coming from her.

"I can do that. At least, I think I can. Nothing is sure with me any more. And it hasn't been for years." Tate's head went down on Timothy's shoulder and she slept, feeling safe for the first time in years, wrapped in his arms.

Timothy was watching her, a softened look on his face. Silver and Naomi shared a look. Timothy was the first of their team to find someone, they decided. Tate suited him. She was who God had brought into his life and they would do everything that they could to protect them both and find out who was after them. They just didn't know who was after them or which one it was.

Timothy shifted how he was sitting, nodding as Mae raised Tate's feet to the couch and then covered her. He was not letting go of her, that he had determined. And he also determined that he would work as best he could to decide who was after her. He frowned as he thought of her words.

"It's sad, ladies, what Tate said. I can't imagine being disowned by my family." Timothy's voice was quiet.

"I can't either." Silver returned from the kitchen with a tray. She had refilled their mugs and brought in the plate of sweets that Mae had left there. Richard and Stephen had disappeared and she had no idea where they were.

Chapter 14

Richard watched Tate closely on the Wednesday of that week. They had packed her into his truck, Stephen and Bill with them. Silver and Naomi followed in Silver's vehicle. He frowned for a moment. She was not acting as he would have thought that she would have. Tate was subdued, not talking a lot, and just existing, he thought. Her face was pale, the dark shadows under her eyes showing black. Richard then looked at Timothy, finding Timothy watching him. They had worked together for too many years, Richard thought, to be able to hide their thoughts.

"Tate? Will your landlady be expecting you?" Bill's voice broke into her thoughts.

Tate shrugged, not sure what to say.

"I borrowed Mae's phone and called her. My room is still there. She hasn't cleaned it out yet. She was expecting me to come back." Tate's forehead furrowed. "I don't know why she would think that."

"Someone may have said something to her then." Bill pulled out his phone, to study the text that he had just received. "We have an officer outside her house right now, Tate. Just so that nothing can be said. The lead detective reached out to her at my request."

Tate paled even more, her eyes growing larger as she took in Bill's words.

"Is she in danger?"

"We don't know that, Tate. We want to have a team go through your room first, just to ensure that nothing has been planted there. Once that is done, then we take you in. You pack your belongings and we leave." Bill didn't want to be there for too long. He had a bad feeling in his gut that something would happen that day. Just what that was, he wasn't sure. He had just learned to trust his instincts. That had saved him many times over the years.

"That fast?" Tate was shocked, to say the least.

"We need to, Tate." Richard spoke up. "We need to keep you safe and to keep Timothy safe. If we can't do that, then you both are at risk."

"They're right, Tate. The longer you are out in the open, the more at risk you are. And if you are at risk, so is anyone around you." Timothy watched with sympathy as her face crumpled for a moment before she shuttered her expressions. "Don't hide from us, Tate. Let us know how you feel. We can take it." He grinned as she glared at him.

"Timothy's right." Stephen's voice was full of laughter as he drew to a stop near a building. He parked behind a police cruiser, watching as Richard was out of the truck and then approaching the officer. He could see the crime scene techs waiting near the building. An older lady stood nearby.

"That's my landlady. I just pray that she has had no problems."

"If she has had, she would have gone to the authorities." Bill was out of the truck as well, heading for the building, disappearing before he returned to the truck. "Tate, do we have permission to go through your room? I know that you did sign consent to that but I just want to verbally confirm with you that we can."

Tate nodded, unable to find her voice for a moment.

"It's okay, Bill. You have that permission." Tate's voice was barely audible. She blinked back tears. This is not how she expected to live her life, on the run from who knows what person or why.

Timothy's hand tightened on hers even as his eyes were on the move, watching for anyone who shouldn't be there. He knew that Stephen and Richard were doing the same. Silver and Naomi were out of their vehicle, walking around the building and then watching the traffic as it passed by.

"Is there usually this much traffic, Tate?" Stephen had picked up on the traffic and was curious.

"Some times it is. Mid-day is usually the busiest. Suppertime is the next busiest." Tate relaxed against Timothy, her thoughts muddled and troubled. "When can we go in?"

"Soon, I would think, Tate." Timothy began to pray for her audibly, hearing Stephen picking up the prayer when he finished.

Bill stood on the porch of the building, speaking with the officer. They were waiting for the techs to finish. Someone had been in Tate's room, that was obvious. According to the landlady, it had been fine the night before, everything just as it had been when

Tate had disappeared. She had been shocked as she had unlocked the door, seeing the tossed look of the room.

"They were looking for something, Bill." Richard spoke the obvious.

"They were. I just wish I knew what. I don't know that Tate will know either." Bill turned as he heard footsteps being him. "What did you find?"

The detective, Mark, looked down for a moment before he looked back at Bill.

"Nothing. Absolutely nothing. They were wearing gloves, we suspect. There are not any cameras in the neighbourhood. Her landlady is changing that, having cameras installed in the public areas that won't interfere with anyone's privacy." Mark looked towards the vehicles. "Let's get Tate in and out. I have a bad feeling about this."

"You and me both."

Bill and Richard walked towards the truck. Timothy and Stephen were outside it, Silver and Naomi with their backs to the group.

"Ready?" Timothy's voice had a question that had Richard shaking his head. He sighed. He couldn't stop Tate from going in. He was just afraid of what they would find.

Bill stopped near the open door of the truck, his eyes on the sky for a moment. He could hear the traffic around him as well as the faint sounds of distant sirens. He could also hear the sounds of nature and just wished that he was off that day and could spend it with Cora and Michel. Only that wasn't happening.

"Tate? Before we go in, we need to talk." Bill watched Tate closely, a down on his face for a moment. "Your room has been searched by someone. That happened today from what we understand. They left no evidence that we can see. Only you can tell us if something is missing or not. So, for now, Mark and I go with you. One of the ladies as well. The others will stay out here. We have an officer who will be right outside your door while you are in it. Do you understand?"

Tate nodded, her hand reaching for Timothys'. Richard stopped her for a moment, his head bowing as he prayed for her. She could feel peace within her for the first time in many years, she thought. Timothy's hand drew her from the truck before he walked towards the house. He paused before he hugged her, letting her go and following her with his eyes. Silver walked beside her, Mark and Bill with them. The patrol officer was waiting on the stairs and turned and walked back towards Tate's door.

Tate hesitated for a moment, her eyes on the door. She felt fear and then disgust, knowing that someone had been through her room and through her things. That troubled her. She drew a deep breath, nodded at the men, and then walked through the door, stopping suddenly as she saw the state of the room. Tears gathered in her eyes as she felt Silver's arm around her.

——

Chapter 15

Tate stared around before tears blinded her. Silver kept her arm around Tate. Tate could hear Bill and Richard speaking quietly behind her before she moved forward, her hands reaching for her clothes. She began to fold them, Silver's hands there to help.

Tate turned at last, realizing that she had packed everything. The only thing left was her Bible. She reached for it from the nightstand, frowning for a moment. She pulled out an envelope, reading her name on it.

Bill had been watching her and came forward to take it from her.

"This isn't yours?"

"No, it's not, Bill. It wasn't here that last time that I read from the Bible. I don't know who would do this." Tate grew afraid. This was not what she had expected to find.

"We'll take. Look at it. And then we'll talk." Bill nodded at Mark. "Mark, let's get Tate out of here and then we'll take a look at this and decide if you need to keep it or if I can."

"I would think that you could. We'll make that decision together, Bill. And you're right. We need to get her out of here and back to Elmton."

Tate walked out of the building and into Timothy's arms. He hugged her, his eyes on Bill.

Richard and Stephen reached for Tate's bags before heading for Richard's truck.

"Bill? What happened?" Naomi spoke for the group.

"Tate found a letter in her Bible. We need to take a look at it." Bill hesitated. "I need to head for the department here. Silver, can you wait and drive me back? Naomi, will you go with Richard? We want to get Tate out of here."

"We can do that." Richard pointed at the truck. "In there anyone who's coming with us. Bill, call me later."

Tate snuggled as close to Timothy as she could. She was scared, she acknowledged to herself. No, she thought, not scared, terrified.

Timothy waited patiently for Tate to speak but she didn't. He prayed for her, desperate to have this over with so that he could get on with dating her. Only, he didn't know when that would happen.

Stephen watched the vehicle behind him, keeping just far enough back so that he couldn't get a good look at the driver.

"We have a tail, Richard."

Richard turned to watch the vehicle.

"It's not getting close, is it?" His phone was out as he sent a text to Bill. "Bill will look into it."

"But he won't find anything, will he?" Stephen shook his head. "How do we do this, Richard? This is all new territory for us."

"I know, Stephen. I have a call in to Abe, to get his thoughts. He went through this with his team. Don's going to be in on the call. We'll meet tomorrow and try and make plans." Richard turned back to Timothy, finding Timothy watching him in return. "Timothy? We'll meet tomorrow. We need to make plans."

Timothy sighed.

"I know that we do. I want Tate to be part of it. It's her life. Maybe by then, Bill will have some answers from that letter." His eyes dropped to Tate's head, which was now on his shoulder. She had drifted off, the lack of sleep causing that.

Richard nodded, knowing that he could and would work with that.

"Richard?" Abe's voice echoed over the phone, knowing that Don was with Richard. "You're ready to talk?"

"I am, Abe. Thanks for taking the time. How many of your team are there?" Richard grinned as he heard Abe laugh. "All of you?"

"Yep. They want to help. You've gone above and beyond for us on many times." Richard reached for his pen. "Now, let me bring you up to date on Tate and Timothy." He did just that, seeing Don making notes. "So, that's where we stand."

Abe shared a look with his team members. Each of them had faced danger with their ladies. They had talked earlier about what they could offer Richard in help, and Abe had a consensus of that.

—

82

"Richard, I'm sending you an email with what our thoughts are. You should have it. Don, I've sent it to you as well. You may need to step in to help. I'm glad that you are in on this planning."

"Not a problem, Abe. It's what we do. Besides, Richard has been a friend of mine for years. We work together well and that includes your team. Now, what do we do? Timothy's in the office, Richard says, until he's cleared medically. He's not sure when that will be, is that correct, Richard?"

"It is. He's frustrated. He wants in on this but can't be. Tate? Now, that's a different story." Richard rubbed at his head, not sure how to explain her. "She's been on her own for too many years. She was kicked out of her home at eighteen, told that her parents didn't want her, and that they didn't want to see her again."

Micah looked up at that.

"Do you have their names, Richard? I can get Kat to start working on a family tree on Tate." Micah's wife, Kataleen, had a family tree program that she used to research criminals and others that she was asked to.

"I do. I'll send it to you. Thank Kat for us. Now, as to today, we went to Holly to retrieve her belongings. Someone had been in her room, tossed her belongings, and then left a letter in her Bible. That would have been done today. Bill's working on it."

"Then, you'll get some answers." Abe looked down at his notes. "Now, if we need to, I can spring some of my guys free and send them your way. If anything, Darci has heard about this."

—

"And she's comping up with a profile?" Richard grinned as he heard the laughter from Abe's team. Darci was a former forensics psychologist and would do suspect profiles for friends.

"She is. She said that they would head your way, likely on the weekend. Doug wants to talk with Timothy, just to see what he can do for him." Abe's cousin, Doug, was the head of the town ETF force.

"That's good. Timothy is chafing at the bit, as they say. Tate? She's gone quiet. She's not sure who to trust right now, given how she has had to depend only on herself."

"We've seen that, Richard, so many times with those we protect. We'll pray for her and for Timothy." Abe sat back as he cut off the call, his eyes on his team. They were all concerned, knowing how dangerous it was for Timothy and Tate.

Chapter 16

Tate turned that Saturday, not sure where she wanted to be. She headed for the door, heading outside and then just standing on the sidewalk in front of Mae's house. She studied Timothy's house and then turned and walked away. She needed to be by herself for a few hours, and that she couldn't do at Mae's. Timothy hunted her down every night, just sitting with her. He didn't question her. Instead, he just spoke with her, prayed for her, hugged her, and then left. Tate was at a loss to know what to do about this.

Her head turning as she searched for something, Tate wasn't sure what she was actually looking for. She just wanted this over with. Timothy was in danger, just by being her friend. Tate frowned at that. No, she thought, he was in danger before they had met. And that she didn't understand at all.

Lost in thought, Tate didn't hear the running footsteps. She screamed as arms came around and a hand was slapped across her mouth. She fought to free herself, her hands grabbing at the arms, her feet kicking at the shins of the man who simply picked her up and walked away with her. Stood on her feet, Tate kept struggling to escape but it was to no avail. A gag was slapped across her mouth and then a blindfold across her eyes. Her hands were tugged hard behind her and bound. She was forced to walk across rough ground before she was shoved down. She hit the ground hard, her head bouncing back up. Her consciousness fading, she felt her ankles being bound before she dropped into that dark well that didn't let her know what was happening.

The men stood, their eyes on Tate before they raised to search the area around the abandoned house that they had dumped Tate behind. They were running away before they were seen. Tate had disappeared and this was what their plans and instructions had been.

Timothy gathered up his grocery bags and headed for his home. Setting the bags on the kitchen table, he paced back to the living room window, searching the street. He felt something off but wasn't sure just what was troubling him. *Lord,* he prayed, *be with my lady. Protect her, please? Help her to learn to trust You more and more.*

His groceries set away, Timothy grabbed his inevitable mug of coffee and headed for his office. The mug hit the desk as he sat, his hands reaching for his Bible. He needed that time on that Saturday, not knowing why, but deeply troubled.

He rose at last, setting his mug into the sink, pausing for a moment. He was troubled about Tate and not sure why. Tapping at Mae's door, he entered, kicking off his shoes. Mae appeared in the hallway, a small towel in her hands that she had just dried them on.

"Timothy? You're here?" Mae was puzzled.

"I am. And how are you today?" He grinned as he hugged her, passing her and heading for the kitchen. "You've been busy baking."

"I have been. That doesn't explain why you're here." Mae dropped the towel on the counter before she turned to Timothy. "I thought that you and Tate were busy today."

"Not yet. I had some errands to run today. Where is she?" Timothy headed for the kitchen doorway, intent on finding Tate. He stopped in his tracks at Mae's words. He spun, shock on his face. "What was that, Mae?"

"She's not here. She must have left earlier when I had to slip out to get the few things that I needed. She was gone when I got back. I thought that you and she were together, when I didn't see your car." Mae paled before her face grew stern. "It's been three hours, Timothy, since I got back. Where is she?"

Timothy spun back to stare at her, fear in his heart.

"It has been? Where is she?" Timothy spun back to stare down the hall. "Mae, you're sure that she's not here anywhere?"

"I'm sure, Timothy." Mae reached for her phone, intent on calling in help.

Timothy was out of the house, searching outside Mae's house and then searching around his own home. He looked up at the sky. Rain clouds were moving in. The weather report had called for drizzle and he was afraid that Tate was out in it.

Richard paused as he walked towards Timothy. The other three members of their team were away, out of town. He stood beside Timothy as he spoke with the patrol officer who had responded.

Timothy turned at last, worry on his face. Richard nodded to himself. *Yes,* he thought, *they are a couple, whether they acknowledge it or not. Lord, protect my friends.*

"Timothy? What's going on? I got your text but you didn't say much other than you had to speak with me."

"It's Tate. She's missing. Mae said it's been about four hours now." Timothy paced around in a small circle.

"Missing? From here?" Richard stared at Timothy, not sure that he had heard him correctly.

"From here. I was out doing errands. Mae had had to go out. When she got back, she thought that Tate was with me. But she wasn't. I have no idea of where she is."

Richard nodded, a hand on Timothy's shoulder, a prayer uttered for him and Tate.

"We'll start searching, Timothy. Where have you looked?"

"At Mae's. Around my place. I was heading for the neighbours to see if they had seen anything."

Richard nodded, his hand keeping Timothy in place. His keen eyes watched the activity around them.

"We need to make some plans, Timothy. Let's head for Mae's." Richard had watched Mae as she stood on the city sidewalk in front of her home. "We'll plan, Timothy. And then do our own search. The officers are aware of what is going on. It won't be shoved to one side. Bill and Andrew will see to that."

Timothy nodded, knowing that Richard spoke the truth. He turned, heading for Mae, fatigue weighing down his feet and body. Mae watched him, reaching to hug him before she turned him towards the house.

Richard waited, seeing Bill walking towards him.

"Bill? I thought that you and Cora were away this weekend."

"We were to be, but Michael wasn't feeling great. And then Jason had to be away on an emergency. So I picked up to cover for him." Bill looked around at the activity. "What's going on? I just heard someone is missing."

"It's Tate." Richard didn't see Bill's eyes fly to watch him. "She's been going for about four hours. Neither Timothy nor Mae realized that she was, the other thinking that she was with one of them."

"And she wasn't." Bill pulled his cap down on his forehead, trying to block the drizzle that had started. "This weather is not going to help us search."

"No, it won't. And I doubt that she would have just run away. I don't read her that way."

"None of u do." Bill turned as a patrol officer approached him. "Head for Mae's, Richard. I'll be in shortly."

Chapter 17

Timothy simply stood and stared out of the window at the backyard. He squinted up at the sky, wishing that the rain had stayed away. This would not help them to find Tate. He turned as he felt a hand on his arm.

Richard had approached him, a letter in his hand. The patrol officer had brought it over, after speaking with Bill.

"Timothy? This was left at your home. The officer brought it over. Bill cleared it." He held out the envelope.

Timothy stared down at it, not willing to take it but knowing that he had to. He reached for it at last, his hand shaking as he did so. He didn't want to open it but he had to. He had no choice.

"Timothy?" Mae stood watching him, her heart breaking for her young friend.

"A letter, Mae. I don't want to open it." Timothy had not heard Bill coming in and stopping in the doorway.

"I know that you do. Open it, Timothy, and we'll deal with what's there." Mae moved closer to him, her arms wrapping around herself.

Timothy nodded, finally opening the flap and withdrawing the folded piece of paper. He had a very bad feeling about what it contained. Unfolding it, he stared at it, not comprehending what he was reading.

—

Bill reached for it, his eyes on his friend. He read what was written, somber thoughts filling his mind.

Too late. Your woman is dead. You'll never see her again. You could have cooperated with us but you chose not to. Her death is on you.

Bill read it again, not sure what Timothy was to have cooperated with them about. And he wasn't even sure who he hadn't cooperated with.

"Do you have anything to tell me, Timothy?" Bill's voice was quiet but questioning.

Timothy shook his head. He had no idea who this was.

"I don't know, Bill." Timothy ran his hands through his hair before he shoved them into his pockets. They were shaking and he couldn't stop that. "I wish I knew what they wanted. You know me. You know my family. You know my history. I don't have any enemies that I know off. I really don't."

"We know that, Timothy. Richard has been going back over your time with the team, searching for anyone who may have wanted to harm you. He hasn't come up with anyone." Bill nodded at Richard.

"We both have been. We can't figure it out." Timothy paced away, heading for the back door and the yard. He slumped into a chair, his eyes on the trees at the back. Mae backed onto a park. He studied it, a thought coming to his mind.

Stephen had appeared, receiving Richard's message. He had simply turned his truck around and headed back home.

"Timothy? Any word?" Stephen sat in a nearby chair, praying for his friend.

"Not a word, Stephen. Not a word. I wish I had been here. Maybe she wouldn't have disappeared." Timothy's worry and devastation were evident in his voice and on his face.

"She may still have, and you would have too." Stephen looked around. "What do we know?"

"Not a lot. I was out doing errands. Mae was too. We didn't realize for about three hours that she was gone. Did Richard tell you about the letter?"

Stephen nodded, having spoken with Richard on the way through the house.

"He did. We don't get that, Timothy. Is this true or is it just a way to stress you out more? To use you to get to Tate?"

Timothy shrugged. He had no idea what the idea was of the letter's author, but he was determined to find out who it was and bring them to justice.

Stephen shifted his gaze between Timothy and the trees. He frowned, not sure what Timothy was thinking.

"Timothy? What are you thinking?"

"I think that she's somewhere near here. They want to scare me and they can't do that if she's too far away." He nodded at the trees. "Would she be there?"

Stephen stared at him and then at the trees. He was on his feet, pulling Timothy with him, almost running for the trees.

"We'll search, Timothy.   Are there any abandoned buildings near here?"

"There are."   Timothy stopped abruptly, his mind racing as he thought through Stephen's words. "There are a couple of small parks as well." He ran for the trees, not hearing Bill's shout at him.

"Now, where are they off to?" Bill stood on the porch, Richard beside him.

"I have no idea. Yet they seem to have an idea of what to do. Any word from your side?"

"Not a one. It's strange, Richard. I don't get it. And there hasn't been any word on the street. At least not that has come to our attention."

"It is strange, Bill. We haven't found anything regarding anyone with a grudge against Timothy. And if it's there, then we should be able to."

"We should. Emma's been away but I did reach out to her. Jace at her office said that he could work on it but he had to finish off an urgent search first." Bill was frustrated. This was not how it was to be. He needed to be somewhere else at that moment. "Listen. I need to be at another crime scene. I'll keep in touch with the officers here. If you find her, let me know."

Richard kept his eyes on Stephen and Timothy even as Bill walked away. He was frustrated, he knew, but God was in control. He had to hold on to that promise. He walked towards Timothy, finding that he had disappeared through the trees. Richard paused, before he shook his head and walked back to the house. Mae was waiting for him, a frown on her face.

Chapter 18

Timothy fought his way through the underbrush, Stephen following in his footsteps. They stood for a moment, looking around, not sure where to search.

"Where do we go?" Stephen spun in a circle, a frown covering his face. He wiped at the drizzle wetting his face.

Timothy shrugged, eying the woods on either side of him. He pointed to their left.

"That way. It leads to a little parkette. And there are a couple of houses that are abandoned between here and there. Or at least they are empty. I haven't seen anyone around them in years."

"Okay, we'll go that way first and then go back the other way. Lead on, Timothy. You know this area."

Timothy paced away, his head moving as he searched. He had dropped into his work mode, concentrating on his task. He could hear Stephen beside him, following the same process. Stephen's hand on his arm stopped him.

"Timothy? That house there? Do you know who owns it?" Stephen pointed at a ramshackle house, the back covered porch falling off the main house.

"No, I don't. It's been empty for so many years, before I moved here five years ago. I've heard rumours in the neighbourhood about this place. It's what, five or so blocks from Mae's?"

"About that." Stephen walked towards the house, not knowing why but drawn towards it. He had no idea why. He stopped abruptly and was then running towards the porch.

Timothy stood, stunned at Stephen's action before he was running after Stephen.

"Call for help, Timothy! It's Tate!" Stephen was on his knees, reaching to untie her and remove the gag and blindfold.

Timothy's phone was out as he stood, a hand on Stephen's shoulder.

"How did you know?" Timothy was astounded.

"God, I guess. She's not waking, Timothy." Stephen was a paramedic and worked to try to revive her. "She's soaked through."

Timothy was shrugging out of his jacket, handing it to Stephen to cover Tate.

"Is she hurt?"

"I can't tell, Timothy. We need to get her help." Stephen was on his feet, stepping back for the paramedics to move in.

A patrol officer beckoned the two men back away.

"How did you know to look here?"

Timothy shrugged, sharing a look with Stephen.

"We were just searching. We decided to walk this way and if we didn't find anything, then go the other way. Stephen saw something and ran towards it.

It was Tate." Timothy walked away at that, following the stretcher and Tate, hopping up to ride with her.

The patrol officer's mouth opened and closed.

"Did he really just do that?"

"He did." Stephen gave a wry smile. "He's invested in her. She has no family here and he's taking that spot with her."

"I see. Bill mentioned something about that. But I still need to talk with him." The officer was frustrated.

"I know you do. Listen, I'm heading back for Mae's and then the hospital. Catch up with us there." Stephen walked away as the officer turned back to the house and the team that was searching.

Timothy hesitated as he jumped from the ambulance. He watched as the stretcher was lowered and then wheeled into the Emergency Department. He was afraid for his lady, afraid that she would not make it. He had no idea how seriously she was hurt. All he knew was that she had been out in the drizzle and couldn't seek shelter.

Richard found him later, studying him closely. He had been shocked when Stephen had appeared, damp from the rain but insistent that he needed to move and move quickly. Mae had approached them before reaching for her purse, shoving them out of the house and locking the door behind them.

Timothy looked up as he felt a hand on his shoulder. He shuddered for a moment, not sure what to say.

—

"Stephen said that you two found her?"

"We did. Behind the Thomas house. She was bound, gagged, and blindfolded. She's not conscious, Richard. I don't know how she is."

"We'll find out, Timothy. We'll find out." Richard walked away, heading for the clerk, leaving Mae to sit beside Timothy, an arm around his shoulders.

"You two just went out searching?" At Timothy's nod, Mae made a decision, one that he just wasn't sure was the right one. "You're in love with her, Timothy. Don't say a word. She hears that from you first. Now, we pray for her and for you. That's what we do. As much as it seems that God is not in control, He is. He has you covered with His hands. Nothing happens that He does not allow."

Timothy had quietened, turning his head to Mae.

"Thanks, Mae. I am trying to remember that, Mae, but it is sometimes hard to do. I'm not used to being in this position."

"None of you are. You're usually on the other side. Find someone who you can speak with. Abe's fellows. Bill. Andrew. Any of the eight friends of Bill's and Andrew's who went through things. And then there's Ashlynn and her girls."

"I know." Timothy's head went back on the wall behind him. He could hear the sounds that were normal for the hospital, including the pages for physicians over the intercom system. "It's hard to become one of them. And there's Silas as well."

—

97

"That there is. You have many who will speak with you, pray with you, and get you through this." Mae nodded towards the exam rooms. "There are people praying for your lady as well. She is loved here, Timothy, even in the short time that we have known her."

Chapter 19

Timothy looked up and then rose to his feet as Richard approached him, a physician beside him. He was afraid at that point, afraid that Tate was hurt worse than she was. Richard sighed as he saw the look on Timothy's face and then Stephen, Silver, and Naomi flanking him. He had not expected the two ladies to be there but they were. It's what they did as a team.

"Richard? Can I see Tate?" Timothy's voice was barely audible. The strain was showing on his face.

"In a few moments, Timothy. Let Philip here tell you what's going on. We've added you and Mae as her medical contacts as she had no one." Richard pointed back to the chair. "Sit, Timothy. This won't take long but it's better to be done where it's quieter."

Timothy sank back into his chair, feeling Mae's arm around him once more. This is when he could have used his Mom. Only she wasn't here. He had no idea where his parents were at the moment. And his brother and his family were away on vacation.

"Timothy?" Philip sat beside him, assessing him. He could see the ravages that the worry and strain were causing Timothy in his face and hear it in his voice. "She's alive but wet and cold. She's been awake for a bit but is sleeping right now. She wasn't harmed other than for being out in the weather. There are scrapes on her wrists where she tried to get away and couldn't."

"Thank you, Philip. How long will she be in here?"

"For a while. I don't think that we'll keep her overnight. Richard says that she's staying with Mae. Is that correct?" Mae nodded at that before he continued. "That will work. I understand that Silver and Naomi will be there as well. Now, let's get you back to your lady."

Timothy walked away with him, Mae beside him, leaving the others staring at one another.

"Now what, Richard?" Stephen spoke for the group. "We can't all stay with Mae. And I know that's where Timothy will be."

"I know." Silver paced away from her team, stopping as she saw Silas and Madigan walking towards her. *Of course,* she thought, *our pastor and his wife would be here. That's what they do.* "Silas? Madigan? Who called you?"

Silas grinned as Madigan laughed.

"No one. We were here visiting a friend and heard that Tate was here. Mae had called the prayer chain."

"That she is. Timothy and Mae are with her now." Silver turned to watch Richard, finding him involved on a call.

"I see. Listen, I'll head back for a moment and then find you." Silas walked away, leaving Madigan laughing at the look on Silver's face.

"That's what he does, Silver. You should know that by now."

"I know." Silver grinned for a moment. "Listen, I need to go find Tate some clothes. Hers were soaked."

Madigan held up a bag, a grin back on her face.

"We had some clothes in the car, brand new, that we planned to drop off at the shelter. They're her size. God was planning ahead for her."

"He was. He does that, doesn't he?" Silver paused, lost in thought, before she heard Naomi speaking beside her. "Naomi?"

"I said that I'll head to our homes and grab some clothes for us." The two ladies had keys to one another's homes, walking in and out as if they were their own. "Mae gave me a key to her place. I'll head there when I'm done. Richard has been back through and said that Tate is awake. She'll be leaving as soon as the IV has finished."

"Okay. Grab my Bible as well, please? Sorry, Madigan, I doubt that we'll be in church tomorrow."

"Don't apologize. We understand as does our church. God puts us where we need to be, even on a Sunday." Madigan walked away as she saw Silas heading for her.

Timothy had turned as Silas had appeared, grateful for him to be there. Mae had simply nodded before her attention went back to Tate. She was worried about her young friends, afraid that something dire was about to happen.

"Timothy? How is Tate?" Silas waited for Timothy to compose himself.

"She's waking up, Silas. We'll be taking her home soon. Only I don't know how safe that she will be. None of us do. We don't know what happened today. Bill needs to talk with her first." Timothy's hand clenched on the bed rail, his eyes back on Tate, watching as her head moved.

Silas nodded, knowing that feeling. He and Madigan had been through a pretty rough patch with a body found in the church and then threats against them. They had married during this time and their love was just growing day by day. He left after a while, nodding at Richard as he walked by him.

Richard stood where he was not seen by either Timothy or Mae. He would need to gather his team and talk with them, deciding how they worked this. It was so different when it was one of the team. He really didn't know how to proceed.

Timothy gathered Tate into his arms and carried her into Mae's home. Richard had been there to drive them, Stephen with them. Tate had roused slightly at being moved and then slept again. They had been warned that this would be the case.

Laying her down on her bed, Timothy moved backwards, not wanting to leave her but knowing that he had to. He was becoming angry now that the worry had passed. He needed to talk with Richard. Only he didn't know how that would go.

He paused outside of the bedroom, hearing soft sounds from behind the door and then sounds and conversation from the kitchen. He looked up to see Bill standing in front of him.

"Bill? What do you know?"

"Not a lot at present. Tate did give me her statement. Not that she could tell me much." Bill reached out a hand to steady Timothy. "Look, you need to get some food into you. And then, we'll talk."

Chapter 20

Tate roused in the night, snuggling down under the covers. She was chilled, despite the hot water bottle at her feet. She gave a cough, praying that she would not have any side effects from her chilling. It puzzled her, what had happened. The men had not said anything. Bill had told her that there was nothing with her. To hear that she had been found so close to Mae's? That was a mystery. And she just knew that Timothy would not have gone across the street to his home. He would be out in the living room or office.

Early morning found Timothy on his feet, heading down the street to the abandoned house. Naomi walked beside him, not asking any questions. He was doing exactly what she would have done.

"Timothy? What's the history on this place? I know that this is your home town. Richard didn't know much about it, either."

"There's not a lot to know about it. The Thomas family just died away, literally. The house has been vacant for many years. I need to find out why."

"Talk to Samuel. He can do a title search for you." Naomi mentioned a friend of theirs who was a title searcher.

"I did, last night. He and Aideen were away, out of the country, until Thursday. He'll work on it then. His dad has weighed in. Barnabas has started an investigation of the Thomas family." Timothy stared at the home, assessing it before he headed around it.

He didn't think that he should be but he was driven to do that. He stopped as he approached the back porch and sighed.

"Timothy? Is that a letter there?" Naomi reached for it, a handkerchief in her hand as she did so.

"It is. That was not there yesterday." Timothy leaned over to look at it. "And it's addressed to Richard. That's odd."

"It is." Naomi pointed towards the road. "Head off, Timothy. We'll find Richard and let him look at this."

Timothy just stood for a moment. He was genuinely puzzled by the appearance of the letter. And then there was David, who had appeared and then disappeared.

"Timothy?" Naomi's voice reached through the fog that he was in.

"Naomi, David was here. I haven't seen him in years. Why would he just appear?"

Naomi shrugged even as she walked rapidly back towards Mae's.

"I don't know, Timothy. Have Emma look into him. I'm sure that she's already doing that."

"She is. I had reached out to her last week." Timothy reached for the letter, taking the handkerchief from Naomi. "I don't like this. Someone is watching us very closely."

"They are. And just why would that be?"

Richard walked towards them, taking the letter that Timothy held out.

"What is this?"

"We found it where we found Tate. It's addressed to you." Naomi moved past Richard, heading for the house.

"Timothy?" Richard turned to walk towards the house with his friend. "What is it?"

Timothy shrugged, not sure how to explain his feelings.

"I'm not sure. I am just so afraid for Tate and I don't know why."

"She's in danger, Timothy. She's also someone that you are interested in. And you know from our work what the dangers are."

Timothy nodded, seeing Bill waiting for them.

"Unfortunately, we do. That's what makes it so hard." Timothy stopped in front of Bill. "Bill? You're here? I thought that you were off today."

Bill shook his head. He was where he needed to be. He frowned as he saw the letter in Richard's hand.

"No, this is where I am to be. Richard, what do you have there?"

"A letter that Timothy and Naomi found. It was at the house where they found Tate." Richard stared down at the letter and then opened it. He frowned at the photo. "A photo?"

Bill reached for it. It was a photo of Timothy and Stephen from the day before, bending over Tate.

"That's when they found her. They were followed."

"They were. Now, how do we keep them safe?" Richard paced, plans and thoughts running through his mind.

"That's the question, isn't it?" Bill walked towards Mae's home, finding her waiting on the sidewalk. "Mae? Is there a problem?"

"Not that I know of. Timothy said that they found a letter."

Bill nodded reaching for the photo. He studied it and then walked back towards that house, Richard keeping step with him. The two men searched the area, frustrated at not finding anything else.

"Who did this?" Bill spun in a circle, feeling someone watching them.

"Someone is out there, Bill." Richard walked rapidly away, Bill running after him. "How do we do this? How do we solve this and yet keep them safe? It's different this time. We've worked together on other mysteries, but never on someone on my team."

"I know, Richard. Andrew and I have talked at length. We just don't have enough information to solve it. And we both fear that it is only going to get a lot worse."

"That's my fear. My team, including Timothy, have talked about this. We're at a loss. Tate hasn't been able to provide any more information. She did give us a list of names and we passed it on to you and to Emma."

"She has. And we haven't found anything there that would suggest anyone after her." Bill was frustrated.

Richard watched as Timothy and Stephen walked towards them. This couldn't be good, he thought. Bill reached for Timothy's phone, his eyes on Timothy before they dropped to the text message. His face grew stern. Things were starting to happen and that could only mean increased danger for his friend.

Chapter 21

Timothy studied the photo and then looked up at the sky. *This is bizarre,* he thought. *Who does this? I didn't see anyone around yesterday but they were there, watching. When do they strike next?*

"Timothy?" Bill's voice held the question that he wouldn't ask.

"I don't know, Bill. I just don't know." He walked away, heading for the house and Tate. He didn't care if she was up or not. He just needed to be in the same place as her.

Richard sighed. This was definitely not what they wanted on a Sunday morning. They were away the next day for four days. They had no choice but to go. He needed Timothy with them. Only, he didn't know if Timothy's head would be where it should be. He walked after Timothy, leaving Stephen and Bill staring at the photo.

"That was taken from the trees. It almost looks as if the person was up in a tree." Stephen frowned as he thought through the area. His hand reached for Bill. "There's a tree there that could be the one." He was running back down the street, Bill on his heels.

The two men stopped under the tree, looking up.

"You're right, Stephen. It's easily accessible. Let me call in a team just to go over it."

An hour later, Bill walked back towards Stephen, who waited near the street. *This is getting old,* he thought. They had found evidence that someone had been in the tree but not enough evidence to be of any use. He needed something soon to drive the case forward or he would have to set it aside.

Timothy stood nearby. He had come back, looking for Stephen. He had stared at his friend when he commented on what was happening.

"Timothy. You're here? How is Tate?"

Timothy shrugged, not having seen Tate as of then.

"I don't know. She wasn't up when I came out." He nodded towards the trees. "What did you find?"

"Nothing that helps. And we need that."

Timothy nodded, hearing what Bill was not saying.

"I hear you, Bill." Timothy walked away, hands shoved into his pockets, a defeated slump to his shoulders. He didn't want this to end this way. He was afraid for Tate, but without anything to help save the mystery, they were at a standstill. Timothy wasn't looking forward to being away for the four days but it was what he did. All he could do was pray for her and for those around her.

Stephen had watched him walk away, knowing that Timothy was afraid and frustrated at the same time. He just didn't know how to help. He turned and walked away, heading for the church building, knowing that he needed to be there. The two ladies would be there, they had informed him. He just didn't know where Richard would be.

Tate roused again, shoving aside the blankets, and sitting on the side of the bed. She looked around, seeing that she was back in her bedroom at Mae's. She drew in a deep breath, reaching for clean clothes and then heading for a shower. Refreshed by the hot water, Tate rubbed at her wet hair before she braided it and then paused. Sitting back down on the bed, she bowed her head, knowing that she needed the protection and help that only God could provide her.

Her hand on the door, Tate paused. She thought that Timothy would be there and that made her happy. She needed him in her life, looking for him when he wasn't there. She walked through the house, not finding him, but finding Mae waiting to simply give her a hug.

"Tate? Come. Let's get some food into you. How are you feeling?"

Tate shrugged, not sure how to answer the question.

"I'm not sure, Mae. I'm not sure how to feel. Does that make sense?"

"It does." Mae hugged her again and then pointed to a chair. "Sit, Tate. It's almost lunchtime so some soup would be the best." She worked away, preparing a meal for Tate, setting it before her and then joining her. Her head bowed as she prayed for their meal and for her friend.

"Mae? What happened? I don't get what happened?" Tate paused in her eating, her eyes on her friend.

"What happened? From what we can figure out, you were outside, kidnapped, and then tied up and left behind an abandoned house down the street. Timothy and Stephen found you. You came back here last night and now you're out here." Mae watched her closely, seeing the worry that Tate was trying to hide. "Have you remembered anything?"

Tate shook her head, struggling to control her emotions.

"Not at all. I just don't understand how it happened. Weren't you here?"

"No, I wasn't. You weren't up when I went out shopping. And Timothy wasn't either. He was running errands. We didn't know that you were missing until Timothy came looking for you. It had been about four hours at that point." Mae set her spoon down, her hand reaching for Tate's. "We looked for you as soon as we knew, Tate. Bill was here and so were a number of patrol officers. Timothy and Stephen had an idea and went with it. Now, in case you're wondering, Richard had the hospital add Timothy and myself to your hospital records as next of kin, just until you could make that decision yourself."

Tate shrugged, knowing that she had no one else.

"That's fine. I don't have anyone else." Tate's focus was on her bowl, blinking to clear away the tears. "It really sucks at time, you know, not having anyone close that I can depend on. You and the others have stepped in. I just wish it had been different, but it's not. God has a plan for me, I know. Now, where is Timothy?"

Mae looked behind her, seeing Timothy working to control his own emotions.

"He's right behind you, Tate. Come, Timothy, have some food with us. Then, you and Tate need to talk. I know that you're away for the next four days, Timothy. Tate needs to understand that you are not abandoning her."

Tate looked up at Mae, shock on her face. Mae had gone right to the centre of her thoughts. That was exactly what she thought.

Timothy's arm came around her as he sat beside her, a kiss on her temple. He prayed for his lady, knowing that she was working through who she was and how she fit into their lives. It was a difficult time for her and being threatened didn't help.

"Timothy?" Tate faced him, finding him very close to her. She frowned at him and he just smiled at her.

"We'll talk, Tate. We'll talk. We eat first. Then we'll spend time in prayer. We need that. We need to bathe you in prayer for safety, protection, and more importantly for peace. That will help you get through the next while. I am not leaving you. I'm not walking away from you. You are too important to me to do that." Timothy's eyes held the feelings that he was not ready to speak out loud.

Tate leaned into him for a moment, feeling his strength in how he held her. Then, she moved back, picking up her spoon to continue eating. God was in control, she knew, and that was all that mattered at the moment.

Chapter 22

Friday found Timothy working around his house, cleaning and just tidying up an already tidy house. He was exhausted. The couple that they had been protecting had been very hostile to them and did not cooperate at all. The team was planning on meeting, to make decisions on where they wanted to go. Most of them felt that they should go the way that Abe had taken his team, to training rather than being the security team most of the time.

He turned at last to his mail, shuffling through it, and pausing as he saw the plain white envelope. There was no name on it, no address, and no postmark. He reached for his phone.

"Bill? Are you working today?"

"I am. I'm on a scene right now. What do you need?" Bill's attention was on the scene in front of him.

"I just was going through my mail. I have one of those letters." Timothy could feel the anger growing in him.

"A letter? Look, I'll be about thirty minutes or so. Then, I'll head your way. Unless you think you need someone before then?" The unspoken question hovered between the two men.

"No, I'm fine. I just want this over with."

"We all do. I hear that Tate and Mae are with friends this morning. She's not home if you were thinking of heading across the street." Bill's quiet laughter could be heard as Timothy grumbled.

"I was. I guess I'm not now. I'll be here when you get here." Timothy tucked away his phone, not willing to call anyone else but knowing that eventually he would need to. Only that was not a call that he was willing to make at the moment, not until he knew what the letter stated.

Grabbing his Bible and his inevitable mug of coffee, he headed for his back deck, finding his favourite chair. He sat, his eyes closed, just waiting for peace to come from God. It would come eventually, he knew. It always did.

He looked up as he heard the doorbell and walked back through the house, setting aside his Bible. Bill stood there, Andrew with him, stern looks on their faces.

"Timothy? What's this I hear?" Andrew looked around for a moment. "It's just the one letter?"

"It is. At least, that's all that's here. I haven't looked around outside as of yet. And I need to do that."

Andrew headed that way, leaving Bill to deal with the letter. He was worried about his friend. Things would start to get worse for him, he knew, and that he wanted to avoid at all costs. Searching the yard, he could see nothing out of order. Timothy kept his yard neat and tidy and that made it easier to see something out of order.

Bill stared at the letter before he reached for latex gloves. He opened the letter, pulling out the folded piece of paper. He shot a look at Timothy, finding him standing there with a grim look on his face. He unfolded the letter, a frown on his face as he looked at it.

"How close are you to a man named David?"

"We were friends when we were younger. I haven't seen or talked to him in probably ten years or so until he showed up a couple of weeks ago. I didn't talk to him for long as that was the Sunday that we had the issue outside of the church. I haven't heard from him since. Is that from him?"

"It is. We'll need to look into him. Jason has done a preliminary look but this letter means that we look deeper. I pray that he's not the one, Timothy."

"So do I, but I want answers. I want this over. I'm not sure if I'm the one bringing danger to Tate or if she's doing it to herself." He waved his hands at Bill's laughter. "That's not quite how I should have worded it. You know what I mean."

"I do." Laughter still coloured Bill's voice as Andrew returned to the living room. "Find anything out there?"

Andrew shook his head.

"Not a thing. Timothy has the place so tidy it's easy to see something out of order." Andrew nodded at the letter. "What's in that?"

"It's a letter from an old friend of Timothy's, a David Long."

"David Long?" Andrew's mind began turning over the name. He nodded. He knew the name but couldn't share the reason with Timothy present. He wasn't sure if he could even share with Bill, given that David was working for a law enforcement office that worked deep undercover. For David to have appeared like this? Something had triggered that and he had been sent to warn Timothy.

"What does it say, Bill? Or can I even know?" Timothy jammed his hands into his pockets, partly to hide how they were shaking.

"You can." Bill lifted his eyes to stare across the room. "We need to get this solved, Timothy. I'm just not sure how to do that."

"Let me know what the letter said. Then, we'll talk. I'll need to go to Richard as well. And he's away on vacation next week." Timothy paced, not sure what he was doing any more other than worrying deeply about Tate.

"Okay then, Timothy." Bill held out the letter, which he had placed into an evidence bag. "Read it. Then we talk."

Timothy reached for it, sudden fear wafting through him. Did he really want to see it? God, please? I need to read this but I don't want to. Does it help to move this ahead or does it not? He dropped his hand and walked away, his hands running through his hair. He stood in the centre of the living room, his head dropped, his hands clasped behind his neck. Timothy had not planned on this today. He had thought that he would do what he needed to do and then find Tate. Timothy wanted to do something fun with her, to take her mind off what she was facing but that didn't seem that it would be helpful.

Bill and Andrew watched him closely, hearing the front door open and close. Stephen stopped beside them, having had a feeling that Timothy was in more trouble.

"Bill? Andrew? You're here?"

"We are." Andrew nodded towards Timothy. "He's received a letter that we need him to take a look at. Only, we're not sure if he's ready to do that."

"It's that bad?" Stephen shook his head. "It has to be. Timothy? Come back here. Read this letter and then we can make plans."

Chapter 23

Timothy walked back towards the trio, a hand out for the letter. Bill didn't release it right away, his eyes bearing down hard on Timothy. Timothy nodded and tugged at the letter, making Bill release it. The three men with him watched him closely, seeing the stress in the fine lines that were on his face.

Looking down at the letter, Timothy did not focus on it at first. His thoughts were on Tate and praying for her. He didn't pray for himself and he should have been. He just didn't think that he needed to do that. He didn't realize the danger that he would soon be in.

The letter caught his attention and he concentrated on it. He drew in a deep breath. This was not what he had been expecting, not at all.

"Timothy

"When you read this, then you will understand that you are in grave danger. Your lady is in danger as well. I cannot go into great details about what you are facing. We are still trying to determine who and why.

"I will stay in touch. You two are being watched. We apologize that we were unable to prevent what happened to Tate. It happened before we could stop it.

"We will stay in touch with you, working in the background. Any information that we find will be forwarded to the local authorities.

"Take every care that you can for yourself and your lady.

"David Long."

Timothy read it over and over, not quite sure what to think. He looked up at the three watching him.

"I don't understand. What does David mean?"

"It means that he is watching out for you. Just why that is, we don't know." Bill shared a look with Andrew, frowning at the look on his chief's face. "Do you know what he does?"

"No, I don't. I haven't seen him in a long time, since we graduated from high school." Timothy paced, not sure what to think. He turned as he heard a tap at his door and headed that way

Tate stood at his door, a puzzled look on her face. She had been drawn to Timothy's home when she and Mae had returned from their time with the ladies. She hadn't seen him since Sunday and was desperate to ensure that he was okay.

Timothy simply reached to hug her, not letting her go. He backed into the house, shutting the door, and not letting go of her. Her arms hugged him tight, Tate feeling as if she had come home. She didn't understand that feeling and had no way of knowing what it all meant.

Stephen reached for the letter, handing it back to Bill. He then turned and walked from the house. This was disturbing, to say the least. He paused, turning to stare at the house. He had no idea where to go or what to do. He lifted his face to stare at the sky, his thoughts turning to prayer.

Timothy turned Tate to the kitchen, to face the two police officers standing there. She hesitated before she walked towards them.

"Bill? Andrew? What is going on?" She waited for them to respond. When they didn't, she turned to Timothy, seeing that he was watching her closely. "Timothy?"

"I got a letter simply telling me to be careful and to watch out for you. Nothing more."

"That's it? Who sent it?"

"Do you remember that man that I spoke with at church that day?" When Tate nodded, he continued, worry on his face. "He sent the letter as a warning. He works for some company that he has not named. I'll have Emma look into him."

"That's all? Nothing definite? Then how do you trust him?" Tate had gone right to the centre of their question.

"We don't know that we can. That's the problem. He could be working for whoever it is that is trying to harm us."

"I've never understood how we met, Timothy. Why me? Why choose me? And why you? Who do you tick off that much?"

Timothy was nodding as she spoke. Tate had once more brought up their worry.

"I have no idea, Tate. We've looked into my past, your past, the clients that we have had. We can't figure it out."

"And if you don't figure it out, then we can't take the precautions that we can." Tate walked away, to pace the hallway, her eyes on the hardwood floor.

Timothy stood where he could watch her. Andrew moved to stand behind him, leaving Bill to answer his phone which had been chiming incessantly. He had to walk away from Timothy, knowing that he had not solved anything.

Tate turned to face Timothy, her eyes on Andrew.

"Andrew? What do we do? We don't have enough to figure this out. It's like something is setting up roadblocks or detours. Do you know what to do?"

Andrew nodded, knowing what Tate was saying and just what she was asking.

"We have some thoughts, Tate, Timothy. We'll discuss them with you as we need to. At the moment, we can't put any of the plans into play. There is not enough information to let us know how deep we need to hide you two. And it may come to that. Timothy, you know that only too well. With your work and your friends you know how this works. Tate, we'll try and keep you in the loop as much as we can. If it comes to it, we may need to hide you two away somewhere. And if that happens, it may be without warning."

Tate nodded, having spent time talking with Timothy and also Silver and Naomi. She didn't want to do that but if it meant keeping Timothy safe, then she would. She would disappear on her own if she had to. She knew that she could hide and hide well. Timothy would search for her if she did. That would put Timothy at risk and if he was at risk, then his team and his friends would be.

Chapter 24

Tate was restless. She was used to working and right now, she didn't know if she should be. She paced inside Mae's home and then the backyard. This was not working, she decided, heading back into the house and grabbing her purse. Tate stared at it, thankful for her friends who had taken care of providing for her. Without them, she would likely be dead, she decided.

Heading for the front door, Tate hesitated, her hand on the lock before she withdrew it. She could see a form standing there, near the edge of the porch. She backed away, a hand coming to cover her mouth and stifle the small scream that was rising within her. Tate looked around, desperate to find somewhere to hide but where? That was a question she needed an answer for and didn't know if she would find it.

She ran for the basement, seeking the door that Mae had shown her. Mae had laughed as she pushed on a certain portion of the wall and a door swung open. Tate had stared at her and then at the wall, dumbfounded at what she saw.

"This is for real?" Tate's voice rose to end in a squeak. She moved closer to peek inside, not seeing cobwebs or dust. "It's clean in there."

"It is, Tate. I can't abide dust and cobwebs. It gets cleaned every week. Now, if you need to hide, hide here. I know that you can use your cell here, if you need to. Timothy and I tried it out one day, just for fun. Remember to find that one marker on the ceiling." Mae pointed to an object on the ceiling, causing Tate to frown. "I put it there the other day, planning on letting you know about it."

"I see." Tate stepped into the room, noting the chairs and table, the small cot, and the bottles of water that were on the shelf. "You've stocked it."

"I did. It works as a tornado shelter as well. I've had to do that when we've had warnings." Mae showed Tate how to close the door and then release it. "There is no lock. Unless you know the history of the house and know about this room, you wouldn't find it."

Tate pushed at the wall, squeezing through the opening and then pulling the door closed behind her. She leaned against it, trying to hear anything. She heard distant noise but didn't know for sure if someone had broken in. Tate paced before she slumped to a chair. The light had come on when the door opened. She sighed, knowing that she would have to stay here until someone came home. And she had no idea how long that would be.

Fatigue drove her to lie down on the cot, her eyes closing. She didn't plan on sleeping but she did. She didn't hear the hurried footsteps rushing through the house, leaving open doors behind them.

Mae stared at her front door, standing open, not how it was usually left. She walked forward, her eyes searching, not seeing anything out of the ordinary.

"Tate? Where are you? Tate?" Mae grew afraid for her friend, hunting through the house, and then the outdoors. She stood for a moment, turning as she heard footsteps.

"Mae?" Richard and Timothy stepped inside the front door. "What's happened?"

"I have no idea, Richard. I arrived home to this and now can't find Tate." Mae spun and almost ran for the basement, heading for the hidden room. The door opened and Mae stepped into the room. A breath of relief wafted from her. "And here she is."

Timothy moved around her, crouching down by the cot, a hand out to brush back the hair on Tate's face. He gently shook her, not finding that she was rousing. He looked around at Mae, who just shrugged. Richard had disappeared again, looking around for any evidence of what had happened.

"Bring her upstairs, Timothy." Mae watched as Timothy gathered Tate into his arms and walked up the stairs. She looked around the room before she closed the door before walking back up to the first floor.

Timothy had headed for the living room, carefully setting Tate on the couch. He reached for the quilt on the back of the couch to cover her.

"Mae? What happened?" Richard had reappeared.

"I have no idea. Someone has been through the house, I can tell that. Tate managed to get to safety, hiding in that room." Mae rubbed at her cheek, lost in thought, before she headed for the kitchen. She had groceries that needed to be put away. And she needed that cup of tea. Richard worked away near her, making the tea that Mae needed and then coffee for himself and Timothy.

Timothy had repeated Richard's steps, walking through a home that was almost as familiar as his own. He couldn't see anything out of order, other than the open doors. He frowned as he looked at the front door. It had not been broken into. Timothy spun, heading for Mae.

"Mae? Who has keys to your home?" His abrupt question stopped her in her tracks

Mae turned quickly, a frown on her face as she took in what Timothy had asked.

"You. Tate. Me. And that's it." Mae's eyes slid closed. "Somehow or other, someone has made a key?"

"Or else they have the technology that allows them to dummy a key at the time." Richard walked towards the front door, bending over to study the lock. "It hasn't been picked, not by the looks of it, Mae. Let me get someone to change that out for you." His phone was out as he called for Stephen. "Stephen? We need to change all the locks at Mae's home. Get the best ones that you can. What's that? Keypad? Yes, that would work. And we need to upgrade her security system. Why? Someone broke into her home and scared Tate. Tate's fine."

Richard walked out of the house and around it, not seeing anything out of the ordinary but he knew that something was. He sighed. He had tried to avoid calling Bill but that had become necessary.

Bill stood for a moment, leaning against his car. Richard stood beside him, his hands jammed into his jeans' pockets. Neither spoke to one another. Instead, they watched the crime scene techs as they worked away. Stephen approached, his eyes shifting between his boss and the house. He could hear Silver and Naomi as they spoke to one another as they too approached the trio.

"Richard?" Timothy walked towards them. "You called?"

"I did. We needed to, Timothy. Is Tate still sleeping?" Richard was concerned about Timothy, seeing the dark circles that were growing under his friend's eyes.

"She is. She told me yesterday that she hasn't been sleeping well and hasn't in years. She's starting to feel safe with Mae and that has caused the tension and stress to relax some. She realizes that and knows her body is reacting to that." Timothy crossed his arms across his chest. "What do we know about today?"

"Not a lot." Bill walked away, heading for the crime scene tech who had beckoned for him.

"How do we keep her safe then, Richard? We can't be with her all the time. And neither can Mae."

"No one can, Timothy. Naomi, Silver. This is where you start training her in self defense. It's needed. And Stephen, you and Timothy work with Mae. Upgrade her security systems. That means more motion sensor lights outside. More cameras. Check her interior as well. We'll do the best we can but without knowing who is after her or after Timothy, we can't totally protect her."

Silver shot a look at Timothy before sharing a look with Naomi. The two ladies had spoken about that very idea and had tried to brainstorm what they could do. They had also reached out to a friend, Emma, and asked her to start or more rightly continue her investigation. Emma had promised that and suggested that they could do some of the work themselves. They had agreed, planning on starting that very night.

Chapter 25

Tate took the mug of coffee handed her, a frown on her face. She didn't remember coming back up the stairs to the living room. How did she get there? It was now late afternoon. She had slept for hours and was still groggy. Timothy sat beside her, watching her closely.

"Tate? What happened?" He looked over at Bill, who sat nearby waiting for Tate to speak.

"I don't know. I was heading for the front door and something stopped me. I looked out of the window and saw a shadow there. There should have been no one here. Mae was out. You were at work, weren't you?" Timothy nodded at that, his hand reaching for hers. "I just panicked, I think. I remembered Mae's words about the tornado shelter and headed there. I couldn't hear much of what was happening but I think that I heard footsteps. I was so tired, I think, and laid down on the cot. How did I get up here?"

"I carried you up. You've been sleeping since we found you. Bill here needs to speak with you. And before you ask, Richard, Stephen, and I have upgraded the security here. We're trying our best to keep you safe."

"Will that really work, Timothy? I doubt it. It never does." Tate turned to Bill. "I can't add anything more, Bill. I didn't see anyone clear enough." She sighed. "When does this end? Who is after us?"

"That's what we're working on, Tate. We'll solve it. But while we're doing so, you are still in danger. Timothy is as well. We will all do our best to keep you safe but we can't guarantee that. You know that as well as we do."

"I know that you will do your best. I just don't understand why. I have nothing in my past that I know of. Have you talked with my parents?" Tate didn't look at Bill, afraid to hear that he had and also afraid that he hadn't.

"We have reached out to them, Tate. Lily is the one speaking with them. They are very reluctant to speak with them. She has had to go to court to make them. That has taken time. She will be flying out to your hometown and speaking with them. We have had contact with a detective there. For some reason, he has been looking for you for the last couple of years. I don't have that information. Lily does. She wants to speak with him more and then she plans to speak with you."

Tate nodded, sorrow in her heart at how her family was.

"That's okay, Bill. I don't expect them to have anything to do with me. That's how it's been. I don't really want to hear their explanations." Tate was on her feet, heading for the kitchen, a sad smile on her face. She was fighting tears and didn't want to cry in front of Timothy.

Timothy had risen to his feet when Tate had walked away, a sad look on his face.

"What didn't you say, Bill?"

Bill shrugged, not able to say much.

"I have nothing to say, Timothy. We don't know enough of why or who to even begin to try and make sense of it. I'm praying that we find something soon, but there's no guarantee that we will."

Timothy slumped back on the couch, his eyes on Bill. Something was niggling at his memory and he knew if he tried to remember, he wouldn't. It would take just leaving it to fester until it came to the surface. Or it might take something triggering the memory.

"What did you remember, Timothy?" Bill leaned forward, his eyes intent on Timothy.

Timothy shrugged, not quite sure what to say. He felt Richard sitting near him and knew that Stephen was there as well. He could hear Naomi and Silver in the kitchen with Mae and Tate.

"I'm not sure, Bill. I can't get a clear picture of what it is. It's right at the edge of my memory but not enough that I can tell you." Timothy was frustrated.

"Let it rest, Timothy." Stephen drew in a deep breath. This was affecting them all in different ways. It was also strange to be the ones worrying about a friend and team member. It was usually other friends or clients that they were watching out for.

Timothy gave an abrupt nod, his eyes on Richard. Richard simply shook his head. They would talk later, meeting as a team. They needed to do that, Richard knew. Given what had happened to Tate that day, they needed to tighten up their plans.

Mae walked back through from the front door. She had not checked for her mail, not wanting to disturb the techs as they were working away. She held a letter in her hand, addressed to Tate. It was postmarked from out of the province.

"Tate? Here's a letter for you. How did anyone know where you were?" Mae held out the letter, finding Tate refusing to take it. "Tate?"

"That's my father's handwriting. How did he find me?" Tate moved backwards away from Mae, finding herself backing into Timothy. His arms came around her, holding her tightly and on her feet.

Bill reached for the letter, his eyes on Tate.

"You have no contact with your family? That's correct?"

Tate nodded.

"They kicked me out when I was eighteen. That's been ten years or so. I moved away from my hometown and across the country. That doesn't explain how he knew where I am. Has he been tracking me all along? Is that why every once in a while I felt watched?" Tate shook with fear, hearing Timothy's soft prayer whispering in her ear.

"He may have." Bill's phone was out as he sent off a quick text to Lily. Then he was calling Andrew. "Andrew? We have a wrinkle in Tate and Timothy's case. She just received a letter and says it's her father's handwriting. He shouldn't know where she is. They have not been in contact for over ten years."

Andrew sighed. This is what they had been expecting but praying didn't happen.

"Has she read it yet?"

"Not yet. I'm not sure that she will. I'm planning on opening it first and then going from there. I've asked Lily to contact the detective out west and have him start a search on a private investigator who may have tracked her down. Tate has stated that she feels that she was followed at times."

"Okay, then. Keep me in the loop with what's happening." Andrew pocketed his phone, hesitating before he walked through the door to the meeting he was attending. They were all puzzled at what was happening.

Chapter 26

Tate was restless that evening, not able to settle down to any chair or any task. Mae watched her, not sure how to reach through to her. It was so different from her police duties that she had retired from. She had been on the robbery squad at the end, not wanting to serve any longer. The work had taken its toll on her and she had needed to find something else to do. She had done that, working at the local woman's shelter. Tate reminded her of some of the ladies who were on the run and wouldn't take.

"Tate?" When Tate turned to her, Mae patted the couch seat beside her. It was dark now and the low lights in the living room reflected back from Tate's face. Mae studied her, seeing the dark circles and fear that Tate was trying hard to hide.

Tate sat, curling up in the corner of the couch, reaching to hug a pillow.

"I've put you at risk, Mae. How do I continue to live here and do that?" Tate was working through where she could go. She knew that she could run once more. Only she didn't want to. Mae had made her feel like family. And then there was Timothy. He had bluntly told her that if she ran, he would run right after her. And doing that would put both of them at risk.

"You have, but we're working through the steps. Richard is willing to pick up more. He also has friends who will step in and help. They have already offered."

———

"I know. He talked to me already. I pray that it doesn't come to that but it might." Tate studied her friend. "How does that affect what you do?"

"It doesn't. We have security at work." Mae reached for Tate's hand, her hand warm on Tate's cold one. "We can always put you to work there. You would fit right in. I talked to my boss. He's willing to work with you on that if you want. He's done a police check on you and you're clear to work."

"I am? He has? Well, I don't know what to say then. Okay, I guess." Tate smiled as Mae laughed. "Laugh if you like. I'm not sure about anything any more." She looked towards the table where a copy of the letter was placed. "I haven't read that letter yet. I'm not sure if I want to."

"You will, at some point. Not tonight. Tonight, we're making popcorn, finding a movie to watch, and setting aside this. You need a diversion."

"A diversion?" Tate began to laugh at the smirk that Mae gave her.

Timothy turned from his front window. His gaze had been concentrated on Mae's house. He was frustrated to say the least at what had happened that day. He turned to his office, sitting in his chair, and reaching for the computer mouse. He had research to do, starting with Tate's parents.

Three hours later, Timothy rose. He needed to walk away from the information which he had found. It was disturbing, to say the least. Timothy stood, watching as the water trickled down into the carafe. He reached for bread and made a sandwich, squinting

———

at the clock. It was after midnight but he still had work to do.

Timothy sat back down in front of his monitor, biting into his sandwich. He felt as if he had gone behind Tate's back but he had decided that he had had no choice. He wanted to help the lady in his life and felt this was one way that he could. Timothy prayed that she would forgive him.

Hearing the tone that signalled the arrival of a new email, Timothy opened it. It was from Emma, asking exactly what he had gotten himself involved in. He grinned for a moment at her comment before he began to read. It was much worse than he had discovered. It wasn't just her parents that were involved but others of her family. A crime family, he thought. How did Tate escape?

Timothy's head went down on his hands, a prayer torn from him as he bowed before God. He begged for Tate's safety, knowing that she was in grave danger. And he was as well. And by him being in danger, that brought danger to his team and also to Mae. How did they all stay safe?

Richard watched Timothy's house. He had parked outside of it, settling down for the night. He reached for his mug of coffee, his phone in his hand. He was working as well, answering questions and emails. Richard's hand paused and then his fingers found the keyboard, sending a message to his friend, Abe, who had a security team as well. Abe had turned to training now that his team was all married. Richard had often thought of that, knowing that at some point he wanted to find a lady to share his life. He had heard rumblings from his team. Richard could not fault them for wanting what he too wanted. They had watched Timothy with Tate, seeing the couple falling in love. They were happy for them but wanted it for themselves, only without the danger.

Richard listened to the sounds of night coming through his partially-lowered window. He could faintly hear the sound of traffic and intermittent sirens from town. This was the time of night he usually relaxed. Tonight, that would not happen. His head went back on the headrest as he prayed for Timothy. He thought back over the years that he had known him. They had grown up in the same town, had met during their time as youth in the church, went their separate ways and then met up again when Richard had set up his security team. Timothy was a cherished friend as well as a team mate. He wanted to figure out what was going on and soon.

Tate snuggled down under the covers. She still felt chilled from her fright of the day. She had prayed hard before she went to bed, asking for this to be over. Only it didn't seem as if it would be any time soon. That scared her more than she had been scared of anything.

Her thoughts turned to the letter and she shook in fear for a moment. She had not read it yet. Bill had left a copy for her, instructing her to read it and when she had, to call him. They did need to discuss it. She had nodded, staring at the paper laid on the table. Tate had walked away from him, heading for the back porch and solitude.

Mae had watched before she turned to Bill.

"I'll make sure that she reads it, Bill. Likely in the morning. She's too stressed right now. A good night's sleep will help."

Bill nodded, frustrated at having to walk away, but knowing that he was needed elsewhere.

"Make sure she does, Mae. She needs to know what they said. And I do need to speak with her, to make plans. This has just upped what she is facing."

Chapter 27

The next morning found Tate up and dressed early in the morning. She stared at the letter, reaching to make her tea, delaying the inevitable. She turned, tea cup in hand, her other hand rubbing at her cheek. This was a new habit that she had developed over the last few days.

Tate reached for the letter, sudden fear driving her backwards from it. She carefully set down her tea cup, her hands shaking as she did so. She was terrified more than she had been. *God, are You there? Are You really in control? How do I do this, God? How do I have the faith that I need to go forward? I am so afraid for my friends, for Timothy, that one of them will be killed. I just don't get whether it's me or Timothy. No one can tell us that. Please, dear God, protect us all. I know that I need to read that letter but I am so scared of what it will say.*

Reaching for the letter at last, Tate sat, her eyes on the wall across from her. It was still too early for Mae to be up but she would have been glad to have her there. She would have been glad to have Timothy there. Only she was on her own, on her own to read that letter, to find out what it said. And once more, she felt the terror flowing through her body.

Her eyes on the paper, Tate prayed harder than she had ever prayed in her life. And she had done heavy praying over the last ten years. She closed her eyes for a moment, thinking back over her younger life. It had never been easy. She had always felt unwanted by her parents.

Tate began to read, not taking in what was being said. She raised her eyes when she had finished, a frown on her face. This didn't make sense. She was scared by what she read. Who would write something like this? She re-read what was written, puzzling it out as best she could.

"Tate

"This is all your fault. You made us kick you out when you were eighteen. We no longer have a daughter. Stay away from us.

"What we do is our own business. You have tried to pry into it. That is why you are leaving our home and our family. We will no longer acknowledge that you are a part of it. No one in our family will do that."

It was unsigned but she recognized her father's writing. She just couldn't figure it out.

Mae watched her for a moment. She had been handed the letter by Bill and told to read it. She was also admonished to made sure that Tate read it. Bill wanted to talk to Tate on the next day, which was now that day.

"Tate?" Mae's arm was around her young friend.

"Mae? You're up. Let me get your coffee." Tate tried to shove herself back from the table but Mae's arm kept her from doing that. "Mae?"

"It's okay, Tate. I can get it." Mae moved away, working quietly around the counter before she was sitting beside Tate, her hand reaching for the younger woman's as she began to pray for the younger woman.

"Mae?" Tate's voice broke through the silence that had settled in the kitchen. "I don't understand this. It looks like Dad's writing but I have no idea of what he's talking about."

Mae nodded, sure that Tate was telling the truth.

"What does your father do?" Mae watched her closely, searching for any small sign that Tate was not telling her everything.

Tate shrugged, thinking back to when she was young and asked what her father's work was.

"I really don't know. They refused to tell me when I asked. I know that he was in business but I have no idea if it is legitimate or not. Does that make sense?"

"It does. It's not the first time that I have heard of something like that. It is more common than you would think. Let me make us breakfast, we'll pray, and then do some digging on our own. I am sure that Timothy will be here shortly." Mae grinned at the groan that Tate gave. "Not wanting him here?"

"He's starting to smother me, Mae. I feel like I need to walk away from here." Tate dropped her head to her folded arms. "I mean, it's okay that he's worried but I need to breathe. And I worry about him."

Mae had come to the same conclusion in the overnight hours. She just knew that Timothy would not stay away from Tate, that he would be there every second that he could. She had sent off a text to Richard, asking what they can do.

Tate reached to help, her eyes tracing back more than once to the letter. She frowned for a moment, reaching for it and reading it.

"This just doesn't make sense. How did they find me?"

"That's what Bill is working on. He thinks there may have been a private investigator involved who has tracked you. They can do that."

"I see." Tate ate absentmindedly, thinking through the possibilities. "If they did, then they know you and Timothy and Richard and the others. They will threaten them, won't they?"

"They may do." Mae watched as Tate sat back, her eyes on Mae.

"Mae? What if there is more than one party involved?"

"What do you mean?"

"One after me. One after Timothy. And they have combined their forces to go after us together. Is that even possible?" Tate was grasping at straws, no sure that she was thinking correctly.

"It is entirely possible, Tate. That is one thing that Richard and I have talked about. His team has been in on the conversation. He had planned to talk with you yesterday." Mae grinned as Tate snorted.

"Yeah, and we know how yesterday went." Tate sat in silence, with Mae just watching her before rising to clean away their meal.

Mae headed for the door as the door bell rang. Richard stood there as did his team. She looked past him to see Bill, Lily, and yes, Andrew walking up the sidewalk. She sighed. So much for her plans for the day, to relax, clean, and bake.

"Where do you want to meet, Richard?"

"Your office, I think, Mae. We'll need access to your computer." Richard's face was grim.

Mae took a look at him, at the others, and nodded.

"You know the way. I have a fresh pot of coffee on. And yes, Bill, Tate has read the letter. She is very puzzled by it, she tells me."

Chapter 28

Tate turned from the window that she had been staring out of. It was nearly noon. The group had been working away all morning, with calls made to Emma as was needed. Mae's printer had been working overtime, she thought, printing off documents. She had been handed multiple pages, asked to read through them and give them her thoughts.

Tate had risen at last, overwhelmed and needing a break. Timothy had watched her, setting aside his own papers and rising. He reached for her hand, tugging her outside and to walk through the yard.

"You okay?" His voice was low but laced with worry and caring.

Shrugging, Tate stared at the flowerbeds in front of her. She sighed. This was not how the day was to have been. She knew that.

"I really don't know, Timothy. I really don't. How do we stay safe?"

"We're not going to be totally safe. Not while they are out there." He wrapped her into a hug, feeling her hugging him back. He held the love of his life in his arms and couldn't tell her that.

"I know. That scares me. How do we keep everyone around us safe?"

"We will work on that. Richard has some ideas that he wants to refine before he talks to us. And no, we're not running away. That would only delay the solution. And if we're not with our friends, we don't know who we can trust." Timothy wasn't just holding the love of his life. He was on guard, watching the area around them, senses alert to anything that shouldn't be there.

Tate nodded, her head resting against Timothy. He made her feel safe and happy. And that she had not felt in years. She frowned for a moment. It had been since before she was a teenager and became aware of undercurrents in her home. She snorted to herself, causing Timothy to stare at her.

"Something wrong, love?"

"No. Something I just realized. I feel safe and happy with you. I don't remember feeling that way since I was a child. There were a lot of undercurrents in my home. I didn't realize it at the time."

"That's entirely possible." Timothy drew her back to the porch and to a seat before he was into the house and back with snacks and beverages for them.

Tate took the mug of tea and plate with thanks. She stared down at them, not really hungry but knowing that she had to eat. She was frustrated and it was beginning to really affect her.

"Timothy? How do we do this? I can't be around you. I'm not safe to be around."

"Neither am I. We'll work through it. I know my friends on the other security teams are working through ideas and plans." He pointed to her food. "Eat. Then we pray."

"I'm not really hungry." She nibbled away at her sandwich, finishing it without realizing that she had.

"Thank you, Tate." He reached for her plate, set it aside and then wrapped an arm around her, drawing her close to him. He looked up as Richard appeared, a friend with him. "Don? You're here?"

Don, a friend with a security team, nodded, grinned and then greeted Tate. Tate frowned at him.

"I know you." Her voice held confidence. She waited for him to speak, hearing the sounds of nature around her. Her hand reached to swat away a fly that was buzzing around her face.

Don grinned at her, not willing to give many details unless she said to.

"You do, Tate. I wondered how you were." He sat in the wicker chair, glad to be sitting down. It had been a very hectic week for his team and he was looking forward to being at home for the next week.

"I didn't get a chance to thank you." Tate leaned harder against Timothy, fear from a memory that she had tried to repress driving her to shake.

"Tate? What happened, love? Can you tell us?" When she didn't speak, he looked at Don and then at Richard.

Don sighed to himself. Tate wasn't going to speak, he could see that plainly.

"Tate? May I tell them?" Don waited patiently until Tate nodded. "Tate was in difficulty in Oak City about six months ago. She was approached by a man who tried to force her to go with him. I was nearby and stepped in. The man disappeared before authorities could be summoned. Tate disappeared on me when I turned my back for a moment. I was praying that you were safe, Tate, not knowing how to find you. I didn't expect to hear what Richard has said."

Tate shook her head, knowing that she had to speak.

"I left town that night and went to Holly. He must have followed me. He didn't say anything other than I had to go with him. I was fighting to get away when you came up. He left but I think he was still there somewhere, hiding and watching for me to leave. I felt so threatened by him. I didn't know that I could trust you. I'm sorry."

"There is nothing to apologize for. You didn't know me. I could have been a kidnapper as well." He grinned as she gave a small smile. "Now, what can we do for you two?"

Timothy shrugged, not sure what to ask for. His eyes stopped on Richard, watching his boss and friend closely. Richard was coming up with a plan but it would take a while to put into place. They needed Tate's cooperation, and none of them were sure of having that.

Richard began to pray, knowing that he had to speak with Tate.

"Tate, we realize that you are terrified. Any of us would be in your situation. You're on the run and have been for years. You have had no support until now. We will not walk away from you. Ever! Now you wonder if your parents are involved in crime. That we are looking into. You wonder about anyone who has ever approached you and their motives. You're not sure why Timothy was hurt and if it was because of you. Let's set all that aside for now.

"Now, this is what the Lord has laid on my heart this morning. He is here with you, Tate. He always has been. He will never leave you. He has never forsaken you. You have seen how a bird will cover her little ones with her wings and protect them. That is what He has done with you. He has hidden you in the hollow of the rock and covered you with His hand. At times, He has given you the ability to fly above the storms like eagles. He does all that and more. Most importantly? He loves you. He always has and always will. He doe not desire harm for you but allows it for His reasons. Whatever happens to you happens within His will."

Tate had stilled, her eyes on Richard, feeling her body relax at his words. He was so right, she thought, in all of that. God really was with her. She not likely would know just what all he had protected her from. That was okay with her.

Chapter 29

On the Monday following that, Timothy scowled at the computer monitor in their office. Richard had land outside of the town where he had set up a training building for his team and had his offices. His home sat nearby. He wasn't sure of what he was reading. Rising, Timothy paced his office, not aware of what was happening any more. Paul, one of Don's men, had called him the night before, just to talk and to pray for him.

Stephen stopped in the doorway, looking behind him for a moment. He was feeling uneasy, not sure of what was about to happen, but he had that feeling something was about to. He prayed for his friend, knowing that he was still in danger.

Timothy looked around at a sound. He sighed. He was not alone, he was grateful for that, but he was afraid for his friends.

"Stephen? Can you talk a look at this? I'm not sure what I'm reading any more."

Stephen nodded, taking Timothy's seat at the desk. He studied his friend for a moment, seeing the changes that stress was bringing to his face. *Be with him, Lord. Protect my friend and his lady.*

Stephen's gaze moved to the monitor as he began to read the information that Timothy had found. He frowned as he studied it, reaching to print off various pages. He was on his feet and heading that way when he heard a faint sound. He spun, heading for the reception area. Stopping quickly, Stephen looked for Timothy, not seeing him. Hearing a slight sound behind him, he began to turn, hitting the floor before he was all the way around. Having no chance to struggle against the men holding him down, he was bound and gagged quickly. He heard the footsteps fading as the men ran from the room. No amount of struggling allowed him to escape. His head went down as he waited. He just prayed that Timothy was safe but somehow he doubted that.

Richard parked near his home, reaching for his briefcase and travel mug. He had been out of town that day, meeting with law enforcement regarding a court case. He was tired and felt grubby. His eyes saw Timothy and Stephen's vehicles still near the office building. Richard would head that way shortly but first he wanted to clean up.

Refreshed and dressed in casual clothes instead of his dress clothes, Richard headed for the office building. He paused for a moment, feeling something off but not sure what. He just didn't have enough information at that point.

Pausing as his hand hit the doorknob, Richard hesitated before entering. Something was wrong, he knew. Opening the door, he reached for the light switch, light flooding the room. He called for Stephen and Timothy, not hearing either of them answer. Shrugging, Richard thought that perhaps they were in the training building but that didn't explain the office door being unlocked.

Hearing a faint sound, Richard spun, heading for Timothy's office. A hand to the light switch had the lights on. A sound caused his eyes to drop to the floor beside Stephen, hands reaching to remove the gage and then untie him.

Stephen sat up, rubbing at his wrists. He was on his feet, searching the rooms.

Richard watched him for a moment before his hand was out to stop him.

"Stephen? What are you doing?"

"Looking for Timothy. Where is he?" Stephen ran for the outside, desperate to find Timothy.

Richard was on his heels, heading for the training facility. He unlocked the door there and searched, heading back towards Stephen.

"Stephen? What happened? Where is Timothy?"

Stephen spun in a circle, not sure where Timothy was.

"I have no idea. I was working on something that Timothy had found, heard a sound and went to investigate. I didn't get too far before I was taken down. You found me as how I left."

Richard nodded, his phone out to call in a report. He directed Stephen back to his house, seating him and shoving a cup of coffee in front of him.

Bill walked towards the house, frustration on his face. There had been no evidence that they could find. No sign of Timothy. No sign of any vehicle that had been involved. He would need to access Richard's security cameras to see what they would show.

Richard met him halfway, his eyes on the building.

"Bill? What did you find?"

"Not a thing. Has Stephen said much?"

Richard shook his head.

"Not a lot. He didn't see who attacked him. And he didn't see Timothy."

"That's not what I wanted to hear." Bill stood watching Stephen as Stephen watched him. "Stephen? What happened?"

Stephen shrugged, not quite sure himself what had happened.

"I am really not sure." He watched as Silver and Naomi appeared, bags of food in their hands. "I was working on something that Timothy wanted me to look at and then he disappeared. I heard a noise, got up and headed for the door. Then, I'm on the floor, gagged and bound. There were two of them. I wouldn't have had a chance to defend myself even if I had seen them." Stephen was frustrated.

"We didn't find much there, Stephen. What were you working on?" Bill had to ask, not knowing if Stephen would be willing to answer or not.

"He was looking up information on Tate's family. He had found something and wanted my opinion on it. I didn't get a lot of time to assess it. I want to do that before I say anything."

Bill shrugged, knowing that Timothy and Stephen had likely found something.

———

"That's fair, Stephen. Share with me when you can."

Bill walked away, knowing that Timothy was out there somewhere but no one knew where.

Richard turned to Stephen.

"Stephen?"

"Richard, I printed off everything that he had found. Copies enough for all of us."

Richard was on his feet, heading for the office, Stephen at his side.

Silver and Naomi watched before looking at each other and shrugging.

"We'll eat while we work, Silver." Naomi reached for the bags of food. "We need to find Timothy. Tate is going to be devastated."

"She will be. She's in love with Timothy." Silver paused for a moment, before heading for the back door.

"She is. And he's in love with her. We need to get them through this. Then, they can start dating."

Chapter 30

Tate paced the front yard of Mae's house that evening, her eyes on Timothy's house. Mae stood nearby, watching her carefully. Tate had not seen Timothy's vehicle return at all and it was now into the evening.

"Mae? Where is he?" Tate moved towards her, stopping and wrapping her arms around herself.

"Timothy? I don't know. He's sometimes late getting home, even working in the office. It depends on what they're dealing with. He'll likely be here shortly."

"I can't do this, Mae. I need to leave."

Mae was shaking her head.

"No, you need to stay here. We need to keep you safe and we will do our best to do that." Mae watched as Tate struggled with her emotions.

"I'm bringing too much danger to you." Tate turned as she heard a vehicle stop. "There's Richard." Tate almost ran towards him. "Richard? You're here? Where's Timothy?"

"Tate? Come. Back to the house." Richard's hand grabbed her arm and almost shoved her towards the house, Mae moving quickly to open the door and then lock it after they were inside.

Richard kept Tate moving until they were in the living room where he shoved her to a seat and then sat on the coffee table in front of her. His eyes were compassionate even though his face was grim.

"Richard? What's going on? I don't understand! Where's Timothy?" Tate's words almost tumbled over one another in her haste to express herself.

"I'm sorry, Tate. I don't know where he is. He and Stephen were working in the office. Stephen was reading over things that Timothy had discovered. He heard a sound, got up, and then was taken down. He was left bound and gagged until late this afternoon when I got home."

"What!" Tate's hands flew to cover her face as she struggled to control her emotions. "That can't have happened."

"I'm sorry, Tate, but it did. We're looking for him. We have friends out searching as well. But we don't know who took him. Even what was on our security system is not of much help. They disguised themselves. We're trying our best to find him." He reached for her hands, his grip warm and tight. "Let me pray with you, first. Then, we'll see what we can discover."

Tate nodded, her head bowing as she heard Richard's petition to their God. She prayed silently with him, begging that Timothy be unharmed and returned to them safe and sound. Only, she didn't think that would happen.

"What do they want, Richard?" Mae's question cut through the silence when Richard finished.

Richard shifted to watch Mae, seeing her concern.

"There was nothing to say what they want. The others are searching around and in Timothy's home. It's a waiting game right now, Mae. It's one that we've played before. Only it's different this time with one of our own involved."

"It is." Mae set her rocking chair into motion, the slight creak soothing to them all. "What can we do to help?"

"Get some sleep tonight, both of you ladies. Then, tomorrow come out to the office. Mae, you're not working?"

"Not tomorrow. And I will bring Tate out there. Leave what you can with us tonight, Richard. Neither one of us will likely sleep much."

"I doubt that you will. I pray that you do." Richard was on his feet, a folder dropped where he had been sitting, before he was across the road, heading for Stephen. "Stephen?"

"Nothing, Richard. Nothing at all. No one has been here since Timothy left this morning." He glanced across the street. "How's Tate?"

Richard shrugged, not quite sure how to reply.

"She's hurting. She thinks it's her fault."

"It may be but it reads differently. That's what Emma's picking up on. She's searching for all information that she can. I spoke with Nathan. He hasn't heard anything but he'll call if he can. He did say that their parents are almost home. They were on that cruise and out of touch with everyone for weeks."

"Glad to hear that they are almost home. We need to connect them with Tate."

"And that will compound her guilt, you do know that?" Stephen gave a quick grin. "Listen. I'm staying here tonight. Silver and Naomi are heading for Mae's, they tell me."

Richard nodded, having already come to that conclusion.

"Sounds like a plan. I'll be in the office. I left that material for Mae. I warned them to sleep but I don't know if they will."

"Mae will make sure that Tate goes to bed at least. I doubt either one of them will sleep. Tate is bearing a huge burden of guilt."

"And we need to relieve that as much as we can. Tell me, Stephen, did Timothy find anything about her parents?" Richard waited as Stephen gathered his thoughts and his emotions.

"He did. That's something that he had been working hard on. I want to follow up on some thoughts that we both had. I'll work on that for a while. Take off, Richard. We'll call if we need anything."

Mae approached Stephen as he stood on the sidewalk, his eyes on her as she walked towards him.

"Mae?"

"Tate is asleep. She's trying hard to stay upbeat but this is really drawing her down. It's a culmination of many years of worry and fear for her. Her body is just giving in and she's not able to fight it any more." Mae was more worried about Tate than she could express.

"We know, Mae. We've seen it to some extent with others. We need to find her someone to speak with."

"I have spoken to your friends' wives. Any one of them has offered to speak with her. And Emma has been in touch. She has a friend who would speak with her."

"Emma has many friends who have gone through things. She has a resource list for just about any emergency or need."

"She does. She gathers people without trying." Mae looked back at the house. "And how are you, Stephen?"

Stephen shrugged, not willing to say but knowing that Mae would not let him away with that.

"Struggling. Hurting. Wanting my friend home for his lady. Confused. Does that sum it up enough for you?"

Mae laughed at his grin before she sobered.

"It does, Stephen. The girls have expressed similar sentiments. Come over early in the morning. I'll have breakfast ready for you." Mae walked away, alert but also praying for her young friends, knowing that it was only God who would get them through the next while.

Richard stood at Timothy's desk in the office before he sat. He signed into the computer, staring at the work that Timothy had been doing before he disappeared. *What were you thinking, my friend? What were you trying to discover? And what did you uncover?*

Chapter 31

The next morning, Tate rose, following her instincts to run. Only she didn't make it very far. Silver and Naomi were waiting for her, having suspected that she would try that.

"You're not running, Tate. Not this time. This time? We'll work through this with you, to try and make sense of it all. We'll do that." Silver linked an arm with Tate, drawing her to the kitchen.

Tate nodded, sitting at the table and reaching for the papers, only to have Naomi move them away.

"Naomi?"

"We'll look at them shortly, Tate. First, we want to pray with you and then go over what you've said about your life before you had to leave home. Has anyone ever done a deep dive into that?" Naomi grinned at her.

"No, they haven't. I'm not sure why not." Tate didn't look around and didn't see Bill, Lily, and Richard appear.

Stephen was off on his own search, having spoken to Richard early that morning. He was heading for Riverville to speak with Emma and Abe, to get a sense of what they thought. Emma had reached out very early that morning, asking what she could do. He had simply risen, walked to his car, and drove off.

Andrew had been away for a week and was distraught to hear what had happened to Timothy. He had spoken with Bill who had shrugged at his questions of who and why. Bill was not working that day and had taken the time to search for Tate. He watched her for a moment before he excused himself. His wife, Cora, was needed here, he thought. She was quite agreeable to come and would be bringing Andrew's wife, Phoebe, with her. Both couples had had what they termed adventures and Cora was adamant that Tate needed to hear them.

Mae stood back, watching the younger people as they ate and then talked. Laughter was sprinkled here and there, not as much as she would have liked to have heard, but she knew the gravity of it was weighing them down.

Cora stopped beside her, a hug exchanged, before she studied Tate. She shared a look with Phoebe, who simply nodded. Tate was appearing to suffer from some of the same thoughts and fears as they had.

"Any word, Mae?" Cora's voice was quiet, not wanting to disturb the others.

"Not yet. Stephen is off somewhere. We're about to start working through what we have. Only, I don't know that we have enough to come to any conclusion."

"We'll do what we can. We have others who are working on it away from here. At some point over the next day or so, we want to get together and combine what we have discovered." Phoebe moved towards Tate, simply introducing herself and asking what she could do.

Tate had looked askance at her, relaxing as she recognized her from church. She looked past her at Cora before she felt someone tapping at her leg. Looking down, she smiled at the little fellow who had lifted his arms to be picked up. She obliged him, not sure just who he was, forgetting that she had met him.

Bill grinned at her, watching as his son, Michael, tucked his head under Tate's chin.

"That's our son, Tate. His name is Michael. He'll make a pest of himself over the day if you let him."

Tate had smiled, grateful for the confidence that Michael had shown to her, that she would not hurt him.

"No, it's fine, Bill. I don't mind. I just want to help though."

"And you can. First, let's sort through everything." Naomi spoke up.

The ladies reached for the paperwork, working to sort it, quiet conversation among them. The men had stepped away, heading for Timothy's house, searching for any evidence that someone had been around despite Stephen staying there. Bill stood on the front porch, eying Mae's house and then the neighbouring ones. He walked away, heading for that abandoned house, walking around it. Richard walked with him.

"Nothing here, Bill." Richard walked back towards the trees and then through them to the open area behind the houses. "Mae likes backing onto this green space. It's large for being in town."

"It is. Andrew and I spoke about it when Tate was found here. It's an easy way to get in and out of the area. And because it is so well used by the area people, we can't tell if some stranger has been around." Bill turned to study the trees and what he could of the houses, not liking what he was seeing.

Richard had been listening to him and then a thought struck him. He paled as he reached for Bill's arm, pulling him further away from the houses.

"What if it's someone from the neighbourhood?"

Bill stared at him in shock, not sure that he had heard Richard correctly. He squinted against the glare of the sun.

"What are you talking about, Richard? You think it's someone from here?"

"I do. I mean, I hadn't thought of it until you said what you did. Now I'm wondering if it is. Who would know about this abandoned house and know that Timothy would search around it? Not someone from away from here. It's not close enough to Mae's for it to be connected to them."

Bill rubbed at the back of his neck. *Richard is right,* he thought. *He has gone right to the centre of it all once more. And just how do we do this, Lord? I know that we looked in a superficial way at the house and decide that it was just available. Now, we need to do further research.*

His phone out, Bill made a quick call to a mutual friend.

"Samuel? How busy are you?"

"Busy enough." Samuel was a title searcher and a good friend of the group. "Why?"

"I need you to title search a house on an urgent basis. If you have the time." Bill waited, hearing Samuel speaking to his wife, Aideen.

"Timothy?"

"Yeah, Timothy. He's gone missing. Tate is safe for now. The house? It's the one where Tate was found. It's been abandoned for a long time. We need to know who owns it and who has in the past."

"Funny you should ask that. Aideen asked me that when she heard about it. You know what we went through. She's worried about Timothy and of course, Tate. I have a preliminary search that I'll forward to your secure email. I have hard copies for you. I'm just waiting for some final research to come through. And Dad has been working on the financials of the owners. He knows one of them. He wants to speak with you at some point."

"Your dad does? I thought that he was away."

"He was, but he's back and has been putting in some hours on this. Where are you?"

"We'll be at Mae's." Bill tucked away his phone, pausing for a moment to commune with his Lord and find solace with the sounds around him.

Richard waited patiently, knowing that Bill would speak when he could.

"Bill?" Richard had to speak. He wanted to know what Bill could share with him.

"Richard? Aideen asked about the house and Samuel has done research. He's sending it to my email. And Barnabas is weighing in on the financials."

"They have? He is? That's good. Now, let's find the rest of our group and get working. I've put off any work for the next few weeks. Don was available and picked up for me as has Abe. It's what we do."

"You three teams work together. You need to join forces in training. You all have different experiences and different areas of expertise. You would have a formidable time." Bill walked away and then turned back to face Richard when he realized that Richard had not followed him. "Richard?"

"Sorry, Bill. You just clarified and confirmed something that I had been mulling over. Thanks." Richard walked past Bill, leaving his friend staring at him before he snapped his mouth closed and ran to catch up.

Chapter 32

Tate looked around as the noon hour approached. She walked away from the noise and commotion and conversation in the dining room and office. She craved quietness but knew that she wouldn't find it at that point. When she would, Tate had no idea. She reached for the loaves of bread and sandwich fixings that had somehow appeared, working away on her own. Phoebe had followed her, knowing that Tate was feeling overwhelmed.

"They're a noisy group when they get together. They work well together, Tate." Phoebe reached for the raw vegetables to prepare them.

"They do. They've done this so many times. I look at them and feel like an outsider." She paused, unable to stop the tears that fell.

Phoebe nodded, knowing that she had felt the same.

"I was an outsider at one point, Tate. This is not my hometown. Andrew rescued me one night from a bad situation and then married me the next day, just to keep me safe. We are in love, falling in love while trying to stay safe. He told me that he fell in love with my picture and could not do anything else but save me. Bill and Cora? Cora's first husband was killed in front of her on their wedding day. Bill's wife was killed when they had been married for six months. It turned out that Cora's husband was responsible for giving her a test dose of a new designer drug. Bill and Cora were high school sweethearts that went their separate ways.

They married during their adventure as well." Phoebe worked away, knowing that Tate had stopped to watch her. She heard Silas and Madigan's voices and was glad. "And Silas, our minister? His wife, Madigan, found a body in the church during a flooding. They too married during their adventure. And you can see how much that they love one another.

"God is here, Tate. Never forget that. While we are working away on solving this for you, God is at work. He is working in your heart, to strengthen you and draw you closer to Him. He is with Timothy, wherever he may be. He will protect him. God does not allow anything to happen to His children that is not in His plans for you. We have a friend on another security team, Abe's in fact. Murphy has a saying and it comes something like this: God has plans and purposes for us that we don't know about. And he's right. God only wants our good. We can step away from Him, go our own way, and then realize that we're the ones that moved, not God. He is our Rock, our Anchor, our Protector."

Tate couldn't control her tears. She dropped her knife to the counter and simply dropped her face into her hands. She felt the breaking of the chains that had encircled her heart and felt the freedom that came with their release. Phoebe simply wrapped her into a hug, a prayer whispered in her ear.

Madigan had been approaching them and stopped, compassion on her face. As Phoebe beckoned her forward, she moved to hug the two ladies. Her own prayer whispered in Tate's ear, helping the healing to begin.

Tate moved away from them, embarrassed for a moment, taking the warm cloth that was handed to her. She looked up to find Cora, Phoebe, and Madigan around her.

"Thank you, Phoebe. This has helped. I have felt so alone for so long, even before I was made to leave home. You have made me feel welcome and to know that I am not alone. I don't know what to say."

"Your thanks are enough, Tate." Madigan grinned at her. "Phoebe gave the shortened version of our adventures. Both Phoebe and I lost our ability to talk for a while during ours. But we are loved by our guys. And we love them just as much. We'll pray you through this and pray Timothy home."

Tate nodded, feeling an arm around her. Lily had moved in on her. She had come to ask Tate a question and then realized that wasn't the time. Tate needed a break.

"Let's feed us all, work some more and then have a ladies' night." Lily continued to grin at Tate.

"A ladies' night? What are you talking about?"

"Listen just for a moment. We need a break from this. We've been working all this time. Sometimes, we just need to set it aside and let it stew for a while as my Pops would have said. He had a lot of wisdom that he passed on before he went Home. And I agree with him. Sometimes you just need to step aside and do something different. Then what was happening begins to make sense."

Tate watched her and then turned to the other ladies, finding them nodding.

"I guess. I don't know what to say. I've never had a ladies' night. What do we do?"

"Never had one? Well, then be prepared. We gorge on junk food, watch some sappy movie that makes us cry, talk until dawn, and pray with one another. It helps to get us through sometimes when nothing else does." Cora reached to hug Tate. "Lily, you and I will do a junk food run. I know Mae doesn't have enough to get us through the night."

"Wait! We can't just take over Mae's home like this!" Tate was becoming agitated.

"And why not? I want to be part of this ladies' night." Mae had appeared, an arm around Lily and the other one around Tate. "We all need this. Timothy would be the first to tell you to do this."

Tate studied her friend and then nodded, relaxing in their friendship.

"And he would. I am worried about him but I understand what you said, Phoebe. God is in control. We can't change anything about what is happening to him. We don't know where he is and that is a worry. Let's go with your plans, if you're sure, Mae."

"I am. I plan on kicking out the guys around four. That will let us get set up. Cora, Michael goes with Bill. No guys are allowed here at all." Mae was laughing as she said that, knowing how much Bill loved his son and liked to spend time with him on his own.

Richard turned as he heard the laughter, a frown on his face for a moment before it cleared.

"It sounds as if the ladies are up to no good." His comment caught Bill's attention.

"They are?" He listened for a moment. "They are but it's for Tate's good. Silver? Naomi? I think you need to head for the kitchen."

Silver and Naomi were on their feet, in complete agreement with that. They appeared in the kitchen, ready to get in on the fun and in doing so, helping Tate to feel part of their family of friends.

Tate walked through the downtown area two days later. Lily, off duty for a change, was with her as was Madigan. Those two ladies had just taken Tate into the group and wouldn't let her say no to shopping. Hesitant at first to put the ladies in harm's way, Tate had finally agreed. She had not had a chance to walk the downtown area. She loved finding the little shops that were tucked away and just browsing, knowing that she couldn't buy anything.

"Tate? In here." Lily stopped her and then pulled her into a bookstore. "This is one of my favourite haunts. Bob always has a good selection of books." She waved at the owner as they entered. "What do you have that's new, Bob?"

"Back corner as always, Lily. There are some new Christian suspense novels from a new author. I think that you'll enjoy them."

Lily gleamed, for want of a better word. Even though she was a detective and solved mysteries herself, she never tired of a good mystery and often picked up ways and means of solving some of her cases. She reached for the book, puzzled for a moment that it only had scenery for a cover and then was absorbed in browsing through it.

Madigan laughed and then pulled Tate with her.

"What do you read, Tate?"

"Me? I'm not sure what to say. I haven't read a lot in the last few years, only able to borrow books from a library. And some of the libraries did charge for membership. I couldn't afford that." Tate was saddened at the thought.

"Then, we browse. We find what you like and buy some. Those are our gifts to you. Mae is in on this. I know that you have been reading her books."

Tate was dumbfounded, not sure what to say other than to stammer out a "thanks". She walked the aisles of the store, reaching for and then returning books. She was lost, she thought, not sure what she wanted to read. Then, she found a book. She had heard about the author, had seen him at a book signing, and listened closely as he spoke with the people there. Tate had to walk away, not able to purchase one of his books, not seeing how his eyes had followed her.

Madigan tilted her hand to look at the book, her face lighting up.

"I know him, Tate. Burnie is a good friend of ours. I can introduce you to him."

"You can? I heard him speak a couple of years ago at a book signing. I have no idea why I was there other than it was raining and I was bored."

"God directed you there. I wonder?" Madigan grew silent for a moment.

"Madigan? What did you wonder?" Tate was puzzled.

"Burnie mentioned one time about a lady who had caught his attention. She had listened very intently but left without purchasing anything. He often wondered what happened to her. You must be that lady." Madigan's phone was out and her fingers flying across the keyboard. "He and his wife live close to here." She began to laugh, causing Tate to stare at her again. "I'm sorry. But he and his wife, Muir, had an adventure. He works for the Barnabas Foundation, long story there. But so do twelve other men and then Barnabas. Each of the men went through some pretty rough times with their ladies when they met. They all had adventures as they call them. We need to get you together with them."

Tate had been staring at her, her mouth open before she snapped it closed.

"He did? And there were how many? I counted fourteen. That can't be correct." Tate's voice was barely audible.

"It is totally correct. Barnabas runs the Foundation and employs the men. All of them work in the community but don't take wages from their employers. It's part of the mandate of the Barnabas Foundation to be encouragers to the community."

"I think that's a wonderful concept. I wish I had had someone like that in my life."

"You do now, Tate. We're not letting you escape from us. And if I know Timothy, he won't let you walk from him."

"Where is he, Madigan? How do we even know that he is safe? Did we solve anything the other day with what we were working on? It's still all muddled up in my mind."

Lily had approached, listening to the conversation.

"We did, Tate. We did. Setting it out like that? It clarified a lot. I've been working on it at Andrew's request. So has Bill. And I know that Richard's team is as well. We'll find him, Tate, and get him back to you. That's a promise."

Tate nodded, soberness on her face.

"I hear what you are saying, Lily. It shouldn't have happened."

"And we don't know for sure if he was taken because of you or because of something else. We seem to have two parties involved."

"Two parties." Tate didn't feel Madigan removing the book from her hands and heading away to pay for it.

"Two parties. One after you. One after Timothy. It's happened before. And likely will again. Come on, then. We have a diner to find and a meal to enjoy. Andrew's Aunt Ev has a diner. Her food is fantastic."

Mae entered her home late that afternoon, finding Tate curled up in a chair, deep in the novel that had been purchased for her.

"Tate? I didn't know that you were home already." Mae dropped down into a chair near her.

"I am. I had a wonderful time. Those two ladies are becoming great friends." Tate smiled at Mae. "And how was your day?"

"My day? You know, it's nice having someone here to ask me that." Mae grinned at her for a moment. "It was good. It's heartbreaking to hear the ladies' stories and to see the little ones who are affected. Our shelter is a real ministry and so needed."

"It is. I have stayed in a homeless shelter a few times. Some were really good and others were horrible. It depends on who is running them."

"That makes a big different. Listen, are you very hungry? I'm not. I was thinking of a salad. We still have grilled chicken to eat."

"That sounds good." Tate's eyes dropped to her book before she sighed, setting it aside.

"What are you reading?" Mae stood, reading the cover. "One of Burnie's books. He's a great author. We need to get him here for you to meet."

Tate sighed, knowing that Madigan was working on that.

"Madigan was in touch with him. He plans to bring all fourteen of them."

Mae began to laugh, hugging Tate before turning her towards the kitchen.

"It's not quite that bad. Only if they bring the children. You'll have to watch out for Brandon and Hagen's twins, Heath and Hannah. They are real characters."

Chapter 34

Richard ran towards Mae's home, the hood up on his jacket, as he tried to avoid the rain without much success. He slipped from his shoes, hanging his jacket in the closet, and then heading for Mae's office. He could hear her voice from there, pausing in the doorway as he spotted her on the phone.

Mae looked up and waved him in, pointing to a chair. Richard sat, grateful to be sitting for a bit. He had been busy over the last few days, finding information that he had confirmed and then sent on to Bill. Bill had called him, asking if he was sure. At Richard's confirmation, Bill had sighed and asked if he knew how much work he had just brought to his desk. Richard had laughed and told him that he was welcome and what more could he do for him?

Setting aside her phone, Mae turned to Richard, seeing the disturbed look on his face.

"Richard? What did you do?"

"Me? Solved this?" He grinned as she shook a finger at him. "Maybe not totally, but I have information that I need to go over with Tate. Is she around?"

"She's not. Madigan came and found her around lunchtime. She is really taken with Tate. They had their Bible study today. Tate didn't know if she should go, knowing that she is dangerous."

"She is but we're not sure why. It's starting to come together but we still need that one small piece of information." Richard grew quiet, his thoughts on Timothy. "I just wish I knew where Timothy is."

"So do I. We'll find him, Richard. That's a given." Mae prayed for her friends.

"I know, Mae. But will he be alive? That's what we're all asking."

"He will be. They'll keep him alive as long as they can. It's when you go in to bring him out that he will be in danger. They will not hesitate to kill him if they think he'll escape them."

"I know. That's what's worrying us." He turned as he heard footsteps and Tate appeared. She looks happy, he thought, and more rested, but still not as rested as she should be.

"Richard? You're here again? Moving in?" Tate laughed at him as he grinned.

"Not quite. But how was your day?"

"It was great. They are such a caring group of ladies. And I have missed out not being part of a Bible study group." She prepared her mug of tea and then sat. "But you're not here to ask about my day."

"Found me out, did you?" He grinned again. "No, I'm not but I am glad to hear how your day went. I have information that I need to go over with you. But first, can we pray?"

Tate shared a look with Mae and then nodded.

"Sure. We need to do that, don't we? I am so worried about Timothy." Her feelings for him were evident on her face without her knowing that.

Richard raised his head at last, his hand resting on the file folder in front of him. He wasn't sure how to proceed. He had talked it over with Bill. Bill had stated that since it didn't directly relate to their investigation at the moment, Richard should be the one speaking with Tate. He also accepted a copy of the material, knowing that he would go over it himself. He just feared for Tate and Timothy.

"Tate, I have information for you to look over. Before you do that, Bill is aware of what we have found. It's a compilation of what we have all been working on, including Emma and her staff. It is disturbing. The thing of it is, we're not sure how it applies to you or even to Timothy. There are names in here that we are not familiar with. I have spoken with Nathan. He is not familiar with any of them nor are his parents. I would ask that you read through it and then we talk."

Tate had kept her eyes on Richard before she reached for the folder. She looked at Mae, who nodded at her. She knew the two were praying for her. Some days, that was the only thing that got her through the day.

Tate opened the folder and began to read. Her heart grew heavy as she recognized names, dates, and addresses. This was about her, she knew. How did she go on and how did they find Timothy? Her eyes closed for a moment before she looked up, straight at Richard. She could hear the whirr of the grandfather clock in the living room as it prepared to sound the hour. Drawing in a deep breath, Tate spoke, fear uppermost in her mind.

———

179

"How did you find these?"

"By searching. One name would lead to another or to an address or a date. We have all the data that we used to search through these. This is a summary of what we have. Bill has our evidence and will confirm it. He has asked that you tell us who you recognize and how."

"It's my family, Richard. My family. My extended family. Their friends. How deep does this go?" Tate brushed at the tears that she could not control. "Did I really bring this to you?"

"You are not at fault, Tate. You never had been. Understand that, please?" Richard's finger tapped at the first page. "Walk me through this. Tell me what you know about each one. There will be things that we could not find but you can tell us."

Tate nodded, knowing that Richard was speaking the truth. She felt betrayed by her family and friends. She felt unloved and unwanted. Her life seemed useless at that point. She felt Mae's arm around her as Mae moved to sit next to her.

"We know that it's hard, Tate. We've been there before. But this will help you to heal. It will hurt and drive you to your knees in tears. But God is in control of all of this. Don't ever forget that."

Tate nodded, her eyes on her hands before she reached for a pen.

"I can write on these?"

"You can, Tate. I have multiple copies with me. Talk to us as you do so. That will let us ask you questions or make comments that may help you to get through this. As Mae said, you are not alone. Is there someone else you would like here?"

Tate nodded, her tears blinding her for a moment. She cleared her throat before she would speak.

"I need Timothy here and he's not." She didn't hear the commotion at the door or see the way that Richard was on his feet, a surprised exclamation drawn from him. She felt Mae move away from her and wondered at that. She jumped as she felt arms come around her, arms that she recognized, arms that made her feel safe and loved. Her head turned as she stared at Timothy. "Timothy? You're here? I don't understand!"

"We'll talk, my love. We'll talk. For now, I heard what Richard has asked of you. We'll work through this, and then you and I are going to have a long talk." He simply hugged her tighter, reached to drop a kiss on her temple, and then took her hand. "Walk me through this, please, my love?"

Tate could not take her eyes from Timothy, seeing the dark circles that were under his eyes. She saw that he was cleaned up and ready to fight for her.

"Timothy? Are you okay?" Her voice barely broke a whisper.

"I am, my love. I am now that I am here with you in my arms. I needed to talk to Bill before I found you. Stephen told me that I had to clean up or else I would scare you. Talk to us, my love."

———

181

The day he disappeared, Timothy had walked away from Stephen before he had turned to watch his friend. He had found something, he was sure, but he didn't know just what. All he knew was that he was afraid for his lady. He needed fresh eyes to look it over. Stephen would do that, think it through, and then talk with him.

Timothy headed for the outside, needing to breathe some fresh air and listen to the sounds of nature for a bit. He walked around the office building, feeling something off, but not sure what it was. He turned to head back for the office, stopping abruptly as an armed and masked man appeared in his line of sight. He sensed someone behind him and felt a hand on his arm. Timothy sighed to himself. There was no way that he could escape, or at least he didn't think he could. His hand reached for the man behind him, grabbing his arm. Catching him unawares, Timothy tossed him over his shoulder and into the man standing in front of him. He then ran towards the office building, intent on getting inside and locking the doors. He almost made it, his hand on the doorknob before he was tackled and taken to the ground.

Timothy fought his assailant, desperate to escape, desperate to make it into the building and warn Stephen. It didn't happen. The second man moved in, trapping Timothy on the ground. Timothy was dragged to his feet, handcuffs snapped on his wrists, and then he was shoved towards a van. The door slid open as they approached. Fighting to escape, Timothy struggled to flee but the grip on his arms was too tight. Shoved through the door and to the floor, Timothy's head went down on the metal floor, knowing that he could not get away. He would have to wait for an opportunity to do that.

Pulled roughly from the van, Timothy was shoved towards a building, a hand resting on his back. He was not given any opportunity to even look around. The door locked behind him, leaving him still handcuffed with his hands in front of him. He spun to stare at the door and then paced the room. He stood at the window, hands reaching for the bars. His head dropped, knowing that he was stuck in there and unable to get away.

An hour or so later, the door opened, with one of the men walking into the room. His handcuffs were removed before the man retreated. Timothy stood for a moment, staring at the door and then up at the ceiling.

God, are You there? I need to know that You are. I know in my heart that You are. I just need to see proof of that.

Hearing a slight sound, Timothy spun in a circle, searching for what he had heard. His eyes dropped to the floor and he gave a brief smile at the little mouse who had appeared. He sat, back to the wall, his eyes on the mouse as it moved through the room. His head went back and his eyes closed. He wasn't able to concentrate well enough to try and make sense of what was going on. Timothy just didn't have enough information for that. He had skills that would help him escape if he had the chance, but he highly doubted that he would get that very chance.

Late that night, the door opened again and food was dropped on the floor for him. Timothy simply stared at the man who stared back over his mask. The man backed out of the room and the door closed, the sound of the lock clicking loudly in the silence. Timothy stared at the food and then turned away, back to the window. He stared up at the stars, praying for his lady. By now, his friends would know that he was missing and would be looking for him. His prayer was that Stephen had not be hurt.

Two days went by with food being dropped into the room and then the door locked behind the man. The third day, the man appeared and motioned for Timothy to walk towards him. Timothy refused, standing with his back to the window. The man stomped towards him, grabbing him by his arm, and shoving him towards the door. Timothy stumbled a bit, trying to keep to his feet. He was propelled forward, to be shoved into another room and down into a chair.

Timothy waited, knowing that he would likely learn why he had been taken captive. He waited patiently, hearing the sounds of the men pacing behind him. He sighed to himself. This was not how he was wanting to spend his life. *Lord, I know that You are here. Just protect my lady. That's all I ask.*

Hearing footsteps approaching him, Timothy tensed. He realized that this was it. He stood, his eyes focused on the wall ahead of him. He didn't turn as the footsteps stopped behind him. He felt the presence of the man standing there, refusing to give an inch. His face was blank. Timothy knew well how to hide his emotions.

The man behind him sighed. This was not how this was to go. He had not wanted to kidnap Timothy, to have to handcuff him and lock him away. That was not the plan.

"Timothy? We need to talk." The man's voice was tense. He knew well how Timothy could protect himself and had no desire to have that happen.

Timothy stiffened, the voice familiar. He turned, surprised to see an old friend standing there.

"Patrick Leahy? What is this all about?"

Patrick Leahy, a friend from college, sighed once more. He had lost contact with Timothy over the years until Timothy's name had come up in an investigation.

"Timothy. Have a seat. I apologize for the way that you were treated. You didn't leave us much choice." Patrick pointed to a chair. "We do need to talk. About you. And about your lady."

"Tate? What about? She's not from here." Timothy sat, taking with quiet thanks the food handed to him.

"No, she's not. But her family has contacts here. They have followed her across the country, watching her every step of the way." Patrick sat behind the desk, shuffling the papers on top of it. "I can't tell you the organization that I work for. That's confidential. But I will tell you that we have had her parents and their family under surveillance for many years, well before she was asked to leave."

"You have? And what can you tell me?" Timothy leaned forward, his food forgotten.

"Eat, Timothy, while I talk. We have a lot of material to go over. And I will make sure that you have copies of it all for your boss. We have been in touch with the police service here but that is being kept quiet. They do not know that we have now involved you." Patrick watched his old friend closely. Timothy was good, he thought. He hides his feelings well and that serves him well in his occupation.

Timothy nodded, eating quietly as he watched Patrick. He listened carefully to what was being said before he set aside his food and reached for a pad of paper and a pen. He needed to make notes.

"I'll have copies of what you can give me?" Timothy looked up as Patrick didn't speak. Patrick has his focus on Timothy before he nodded.

"We will, Timothy. I don't need to tell you that this is very dangerous for Tate. They know where she is and why. They don't care if anyone who gets in the way gets hurt."

"Then, what do we do? I need to speak with Richard and my team members."

"We'll get you back to them. But first, let's go through everything that we have and what we can give you."

———

Timothy nodded, sitting back in the chair and lifting his heart in prayer for resolution of this problem and a quick resolution at that.

Chapter 36

Timothy rose to pace, his thoughts muddled for a moment. He spun to stare at Patrick, still not trusting him. He talked a good talk, Timothy thought, presenting information in a compact way, but there was just something that Timothy did not trust. He just couldn't put his finger on it.

Back in his cell, the door locked behind him once more, Timothy paced once more. He felt that was all that he had been doing in the last few days. He walked towards the door in the early morning, turning the knob, surprised to see the door moving towards him. Timothy paused, before he crept through the hall heading for an outside door. He cautionly opened it, peeking out to see if anyone was around. Not seeing anyone, he walked quickly away, heading for the farmer's fields that were around him. Picking up his pace, he began to run through the fields, careful of the sprouting crops. He paused as he exited the field, turning to look behind him. Timothy breathed a sigh of relief. He was free. Now he just had to find his way home. He wasn't sure where he was.

Walking along the gravel road, Timothy grew tired. The day was warming up and he had no water with him. He paused for a moment, heading to sit under a tree, hoping the rest would refresh him. The lack of sleep and the stress that he had been under caught up with him. He slept, not hearing the traffic on the road.

———

One car stopped, the man watching Timothy for a few moments. He was out of the car, walking towards the younger man. He reached to shake Timothy's shoulder. Timothy roused somewhat, stumbling to his feet and then to the car. He slumped into the seat, asleep before the man had regained his own seat.

Late that evening, Timothy roused, frowning at the low lighting in the room. He sat up, his head spinning for a moment. He shoved away the blankets, pausing for a moment to finger them. On his feet, he headed for the door, opening it. He looked around in surprise. He was in a cabin now, not the old building. He was free to move around.

A sound beside him had him spinning, a hand out to brace himself on the wall.

"Timothy. You're awake. Come. I have food ready for you." The man reached out a hand to draw Timothy to the table, seating him and then setting food in front of him. "Eat. Then I'll explain what I can."

Timothy nodded, reaching for the spoon to start eating. He paused as he finished, finding his bowl removed and a sandwich set in front of him. He looked up, a frown on his face.

"I know you." His voice was quiet but confident.

"You do, Timothy. I've known you for years. I am a friend of your father's."

"You are, Isaac Fowler. And thank you. I just don't understand how I ended up here."

"I've been watching for you. I knew that you were missing. I found you this morning, sitting under a tree not far from here. I brought you here, fed you, and then you slept. Now, finish off your meal. I have reached out to Bill and he is on his way out here."

"Bill is? What happened to Patrick?"

"Patrick? Is he the one who held you?" At Timothy's nod, Isaac sat back. He had been following Patrick for a number of years, knowing that he was not as legitimate as he portrayed himself.

"Patrick. I haven't seen him in years. I didn't get a good sense that he was on the right side of the law."

"He isn't, Timothy. He was fishing for information from you."

"I thought that. I was very careful with what I said. He said that he had spoken with Bill."

"And he hasn't. That was to get you to trust him." Isaac rose to clear the table, coming back to set a badge in front of Timothy. "This is who I work for, Timothy. I have worked for them for years. Your father is aware of that."

"He is? He has always spoken highly of you." Timothy fingered the badge before shoving it back to Isaac. "So, where do we go from here, Isaac?"

"We work through what I have. Bill said he'll be out in the morning. I am to keep you safe until then." Patrick reached for the folders that he had set to one side.

"Bill trusts you." It was a statement, not a question.

"He does, Timothy. We've worked together before, only in the shadows as they say. Now, I know that you're a praying man. And so am I. Let's pray, Timothy. This is where it gets very dangerous for yourself and your lady."

"My lady?" Timothy stared at him.

"Your lady. Tate. She's grieving you, Timothy. We need to get you two back together." Isaac watched Timothy's eyes close before he spoke again. "She's safe for now, Timothy. Richard and his team have seen to that. And Stephen is okay. He was bound that day but didn't suffer any other harm."

Timothy drew in a deep breath. He had been afraid that Stephen had been injured or killed.

"Thank you, Isaac. I was worried about him."

"And they are worried about you as well. Now, let's set this aside for a moment." Isaac's head was bowed as he prayed, hearing Timothy pick up the prayer when he finished.

Timothy rose at last, walking around the cabin. It was comfortable, he thought, a place that was home. He turned to watch Isaac.

"Where's Ruth?"

"Ruth? She's away at a conference this week. She'll be back on Friday. By then, we'll have you back with your family and friends."

———

Timothy nodded, knowing that Isaac would do just that. He sat once more, reaching for the folders, opening the top one and beginning to read. He was deep into his work, not hearing Isaac moving around.

Isaac stood and watched his young friend, praying for his safety. He knew that this was when it became very dangerous for him and also for his friends. No one would step back from him. He paused as he thought of David, knowing that David was no longer alive. Patrick had seen to that. It saddened him that this has happened but he had been unable to prevent it.

Walking outside, he stood and stared at the night sky. He needed that quiet for a moment. He turned to look back at the cabin, knowing that Timothy would not rest until he understood everything that was in front of him.

Chapter 37

Bill walked towards the cabin the next morning, fatigue dogging his steps. He had not been home that night and just needed to sleep. That would not be happening that day, he knew. There were just too many investigations on the go.

Isaac waited for him, a hand out to shake Bill's. He pointed around the cabin, not saying anything.

"How is he, Isaac?" Bill spoke as he stopped at the back of the cabin.

"He's hurting, Bill. He's been betrayed by a friend. He found out that another friend has been killed by that first friend. He's worrying about his lady. Timothy feels lost and alone. And we can't change that for him. None of us can."

Bill nodded.

"We can't, but we'll do what we can to alleviate his worry. You have our thanks for rescuing him."

Isaac gave a quick grin.

"He saved himself. I just happened to find him."

"And if you hadn't found him, he may well be dead by now. We're working through that group that Patrick is part of. It's a very vicious group. And it is connected to Tate's family."

"That's what I have discovered. Now, let's get you in the cabin. You can get his statement and then get him home."

Bill stood for a moment, his eyes on Timothy before he moved forward to set his briefcase on the table. Timothy jumped, his eyes rising to Bill, who he had not heard enter the cabin.

"Bill? You're here?"

"I am, Timothy. I need to get your statement. Then, we'll talk." Bill sat, his pen and paper out, ready to hear what Timothy had to say.

Timothy gave a concise statement of what had happened to him, not embellishing it at all. Bill nodded, appreciating the fact that Timothy was so factual.

"Bill? Tate? How is she?" Timothy's voice was tentative, not his usual strong confident one.

"She's fine, Timothy. Your team and Mae are taking care of her. Cora, Madigan, and Phoebe have moved in on her, sharing their stories, and just trying to help her find the strength that she needs. Once we get you two back together, it will help."

"I've been so worried about her. I found something that day and Stephen was looking over it." Timothy paused, still worried about his friend. "You're sure that Stephen is fine?"

"He is, Timothy. Richard found him a couple of hours after you disappeared. He wasn't able to free himself." Bill stared down at his notes. "Now, Timothy, talk to me. Tell me what you found. I have the documents that Stephen had printed. But I need to hear your thoughts of why you were looking for what you did."

Timothy nodded, having expected that question. He just wasn't sure how to respond.

"I'm not sure what I was looking for. Something about the whole thing has troubled me all along. It just didn't make sense that Tate was just kicked out of her home. I started researching her family. Everyone has been saying that they are criminals. I don't see that. What I found is that her parents were scared for her, scared enough to chase her away from her home. I think that they have had people following her over the years, just ensuring that she was safe. Lily has headed out there to speak with the detective. They are planning on speaking with her parents. I am not sure that Tate will ever want to speak with them."

"I know. She has been treated so unfairly. She has seen things on the street that no young lady should have ever seen." Timothy grew sad. He had talked with Tate about that. He gathered a lot from what she didn't say.

"She has. Now that she has you in her life, that will change. Now, Timothy, what are your thoughts?"

Timothy nodded, knowing that he had to speak. Only, when he spoke, it would change things for him and for his family. He shared a look with Isaac. These two men had spoken of the facts over the night before Isaac had sent Timothy to his rest. Isaac had not sought his own bed. Instead, he had spent the night in his rocking chair, praying for his young friend, his family, and his lady.

Bill sat back at last, his thoughts troubled. Timothy had found a lot of facts that were missing.

Bill studied his friend, watching as Timothy ruffled his hand through his hair once more. He could see the fatigue in him. He rose, packing away what he had into his briefcase. A hand on Timothy's shoulder stopped the other man in his work.

Timothy looked up, a frown on his face before his attention went back to what he had just discovered. He sat back, his pen tapping for a moment, before he looked back up at Bill.

"You're ready to leave."

"When you are. We need to get on the road shortly, though." Bill waited patiently, knowing that Timothy would speak when he was able to.

"I need to talk to Richard and then Emma. I have to confirm some things, Bill. This is far deeper than we thought."

"We know that, Timothy. We have some of this information. Stephen passed on what you had found. We've verified it all. We just need to bring it all together."

"And this is where it gets dangerous, isn't it?" Timothy was on his feet, tidying his stacks of papers, taking with thanks the large envelope that Patrick handed him. "Patrick?"

"It's okay, Timothy. I'll be okay. No one knows that you are here. Bill comes out here every once in a while so it's not unusual."

Timothy nodded, still troubled for Tate. He sighed. He was worrying and doing God's job for Him. *God, please protect my lady. I can see us spending the rest of our lives together, but we need to get through this first. And I don't see how we can manage that. We've tracked the lower levels of employees. We suspect the head ones. Until we prove that, we are in danger. And I don't want that for my lady love.*

Chapter 38

Stephen watched from Timothy's porch as Timothy walked towards him. He could see the fatigue in how he was moving. He shook his head at Bill, knowing that Timothy would want to be across the street as soon as he could.

"Timothy?" Stephen's voice caught at the edges of Timothy's thoughts.

"Stephen? You're okay?" Timothy reached to hug his friend before he walked into his house.

"I am. And you?" Stephen spoke as he and Bill followed Timothy.

Timothy shrugged, not quite sure what to say.

"I am, I think. I need to get cleaned up though." He walked away, heading for clean clothes, a shower, and a shave.

Bill watched him before he spoke, his thoughts still troubled for their friend.

"He's hurting, Stephen. He's found out an old friend killed another friend. That has to hurt."

"It does. David?" Stephen spoke the name quietly even as he moved towards the kitchen.

"That's right. He's dead. Did Timothy ever speak of a Patrick?"

Stephen paused to think through the years of conversation with his friend before he shook his head.

"Not that I recall. Is he the one?"

"He is the one who killed David. He is also the one who took Timothy and had you assaulted. Now, we need to come to a resolution of this." Bill stepped to where he could see through the door and across the street to Mae's. "Where's Richard?"

"At Mae's. They're working through what they can. Richard said that they did have information for you and he would be looking for you at some point today."

Bill sighed, feeling his phone vibrating.

"Listen, I need to run. Keep close to Timothy. He's still in danger. And so is Tate. We're moving up the chain of command in the ones after them. We have thoughts as to who the leaders are but need to confirm that." Bill was away before Stephen could speak.

Timothy watched Bill walk away and then turned back to Stephen.

"What aren't you saying, Stephen?"

Stephen shrugged, not sure how much Timothy knew.

"We need to talk, Timothy, and do that before you head across the street to find Tate. She's fine. The ladies, including Silver and Naomi, have taken her into their group. They had a ladies' night last night over at Mae's. Silver said that it helped take Tate's mind off what she was going through." Stephen stared down at the floor before he lifted his eyes to study his friend's. "She missed you, Timothy. Tate has worried herself almost sick not knowing where you were."

Timothy nodded, knowing that would have been how he would have reacted had the places been reversed.

"What did you come up with, Stephen?" He reached for a mug and then the coffee carafe.

"What you had. I confirmed it. Emma has weighed in. She's sending Jace over with more information for us. He's to be by late this afternoon. She just had to confirm a few more details and names."

"I'm glad that she's on our side. I would hate to think what it would be like if she was working for the criminals." Timothy grinned for a moment at Stephens' laugh.

"Yeah, you're right there." Stephen set aside his mug, turned off the coffee pot, and pointed towards the door. "Let's find your lady, Timothy. You two have been apart for too many days."

Timothy hesitated before he followed Stephen. His fear was growing deeper and deeper. He just didn't know how to protect Tate without smothering her. He knew that she would never allow that.

Stepping into Mae's house, he could hear the conversation from the kitchen. He toed off his sneakers and set them aside. Straightening back up, he still hesitated before he walked towards the voices. Richard was on his feet as he saw Timothy. Mae looked up, surprise and then joy on her face as she rose to hug him and then moved from her chair. Timothy hesitated for a moment before he sat, his arms reaching to hungrily gather his lady love close to him. He blinked back tears as Tate looked up in surprise and then happiness.

Timothy looked around at his friends and sighed. This was difficult, he knew. He had thoughts that he needed to bring up but wasn't sure if he even should.

"Timothy?" Richard's voice brought Timothy's head around to face him. "You're okay?"

Timothy nodded.

"I think so. I wasn't hurt. It was bizarre though." He explained what had transpired, knowing that Richard would want a more detailed account from him later.

"It sounds as if it was." Richard shuffled his papers, suddenly not wanting to go forward with the search, not at that time. "Mae, we'll get out of your hair. I have a meeting later this morning. Timothy, we'll meet this afternoon, all of us. We need to do that."

Timothy nodded, not moving from where he sat and not letting go of Tate. Tate simply sat, content to be held, happy that her fellow was back, but still afraid. She wanted details on what had happened to Timothy but wasn't sure that she wanted to hear the details. Somehow, she knew that it would change her life too.

Timothy watched the conflicting emotions cross Tate's face. He sighed. He was here, his love was in his arms, and they were still in danger. How did they get away from all this?

Mae stood for a moment before she approached, her hands resting on the younger couple's heads before she prayed for them. This is where it got difficult, she knew. She had seen it too many times.

Tate rose at last, not wanting to but knowing that she had to. She had to keep busy or she would allow the terror just to grow deeper inside her. She had trust in God that He was in control. Only she didn't see how this would resolve without one of them being either hurt or killed.

Timothy stood at the living room window, his eyes on his house. A thoughtful look covered his face. He wasn't sure now that he was doing the right thing. He jumped slightly as he felt a hand on his back and simply swept Tate close to him. They stood, not speaking, content to be with one another.

Chapter 39

Timothy slumped into his chair that evening. Richard and the rest of the team scattered around his living room. He was exhausted, fatigued to the very core of his bones, but still needed to debrief with his team. He watched Richard as Richard sorted through files, knowing that Richard would speak when he was ready. They had spent time in prayer, something that they always did to start any meeting.

Silver shared a look with Naomi. They had spent more time with Tate that afternoon, finding her agitated and unable to tell them why. They had prayed with her but didn't think that it had really helped. Tate had herself worked up too much for that.

Stephen sat silent, his eyes closed as he thought through what they had been through over the years. Was there someone out there that was after Richard? He had talked at length with Bill and Andrew on that. Both men had agreed that it was entirely possible. They had seen in before. But when they asked if he had any proof, he had to shake his head. It was just an impression that he had.

"Timothy? Okay. Talk to us. Tell us in detail what happened. What the place was like. Who was with you. I know you've given your statement to Bill, but I also know that you would not have gone into that kind of detail." Richard's pen was posed over a pad of paper.

Timothy nodded, knowing what Richard was asking. It was as if they were going in to assess a building for safety.

"There were two men who nabbed me that day. I was shoved into a van and couldn't rise. At the building, I was shoved into a cell, with bars on the window. They left me handcuffed for a while before they removed them. Two days later is when Patrick showed up. He talked good but I don't trust him. He gave me information that when I looked through it and really studied it? It made no sense. I don't know that it was supposed to. For some reason the door was unlocked the next morning. I walked away, Isaac found me, and then Bill arrived on the scene.

"The building was out in the country, about twenty miles from here. Well taken care of. It didn't seem to be the type of place that would house a jail cell, but it did."

Stephen had researched the address, pulling in Samuel to help. They had not liked what hd been discovered.

"Tate's parents own it. Samuel has confirmed that they are listed on the deed."

Timothy nodded slowly, having come to that conclusion. He just wondered how far and how deep it went.

"So if they own it, how does that happen?" Naomi reached for the papers that Richard was handing around.

"I don't know. This is just so bizarre. We're missing a piece of information that would solve this. What is that piece?" Silver rose to pace, reading through her paperwork. A name caught her eye and she halted her steps. She turned, finding Stephen watching her. "This name? Timothy?"

"Which name?" He rose to approach Silver, following her finger as it moved along a line of printing. "That name? I'm not sure. They're from this area." He spun, reaching for other paperwork. "Here. This is what Samuel found out about that abandoned house. It's the same person."

Richard nodded, having come to the same conclusion.

"I think Bill had picked up on that. I know that Emma had. Now, we need to make some plans to trap this person." Richard was back in his chair, his pen in hand, his keen eyes on his team. "Start talking, people. We need to start working through this and making a plan. Timothy, this is your life that is at stake and also Tate's life."

They worked away for the next few hours, plans come up with and then discarded. Richard sat back at last, nodding. They had come up with something. He just didn't think that Andrew or Bill would go for it.

"Who gets to talk to Bill?" Timothy grinned at Richard. "I nominate you, seeing as you're the leader here."

Richard grinned back, nodding. He was willing to do that. He glanced at his watch.

"It will be tomorrow. Let's head out, people. Timothy needs to rest. This is where the rubber hits the road and we'll be not getting as much sleep as we'll need. We know the drill."

Timothy walked through his house, ensuring that it was locked up for the night, and then heading for his bed. He changed to his night clothes and sank beneath the covers, asleep before he even realized that he was in bed.

Tate tossed and turned for a few hours before she rose. She knew that she would not sleep. Timothy had not come back the night before but she really didn't expect him to. She curled up on the couch, a blanket wrapped around her, her thoughts muddled. Tate slept at last, her dreams troubled.

Mae watched from the kitchen doorway later that night. She had heard Tate rise and move through the house before she slept. Mae was troubled. She knew that things were coming to a head. Only she didn't know who or why was behind this. She just knew that danger was fast approaching them.

Bill walked through the police department building, heading for his office. He was in early that day, too many cases waiting on his desk. He turned as he heard his name called.

"Lily? You're back?"

"I am." Lily held up a stack of folders. "I have information that we didn't have and should have. This is game changing, I think."

"Okay. Head for my office. I'll grab our coffee. I heard that someone had done a bakery run. I'll see what's there."

Lily sat back in her chair, her eyes on the folders. She had to talk with both Bill and Andrew. Then she had to find Timothy and Tate. They were connected in a way that no one would have thought. She had talked with Timothy's father the night before, drawing information from him. He had beens surprised to hear from her but not surprised to hear her questions. He told her that he had been expecting something like that for years. He just never put much importance on it.

Chapter 40

Tate stared at Lily later that morning before her gaze shifted to Bill. He simply stared back at her. They were here for a reason. She just didn't think that she would like what they had to say. She felt someone sit beside her on the couch and then an arm around her. Timothy had found her. She was grateful for that but scared as well. *How do we do this, Lord? We need Your protection over the next couple of days. It's coming to an end. We will solve this without any harm or will someone else die because of it?*

Timothy tilted his head to watch Tate's face, seeing the conflicting emotions on her face.

"Bill, what do you have to say?" Timothy saw his team members entering and finding seats. Mae sat on the other side of Tate.

"Tate. Timothy. We know who it is that has been behind this. And you are correct when you say two parties. One party is still in the shadows. We don't have enough information to decide who that is. That we will continue to work on until we solve this.

"As to who is behind this? We are sure that we have identified everyone who has been involved. We can't name them as yet, not until we arrest them. That should happen in the next two or three days. Once we have done that, we will sit down with you both and discuss it. At the moment, you two are still very much in danger. We ask that you take as many precautions as you can but we also know that we can't keep you under lock and key."

Timothy kept his eyes on Tate who had turned her face up to look at them. Silent communication passed between the two. Timothy nodded, waiting for Tate to speak.

"Bill, how deep are my parents involved in this?" Tate waited patiently for Bill to answer, knowing that she had put him on the spot.

Bill nodded, knowing what Tate was asking.

"We're still determining exactly what their involvement is. The house where Timothy was held does belong to them. The abandoned house where you were found? It belongs to a numbered company that they are partners in. We don't know why or how that was used. We don't know if you were the original target or not. And we don't know how Timothy became involved, other than he was there at the beginning of all this. We're still finding information. We do have the search warrants and arrest warrants ready."

Tate nodded. She understood that there was a process but she was frustrated. She had been through enough in her life. She snuggled closer to Timothy, knowing that their time together was coming to an end. Tate was planning on moving on once Timothy was safe. That saddened her. He had made her feel special and loved in a way that no one else ever had.

Timothy rose when Bill and Lily did, walking out with them. He was frustrated, he knew, but it wasn't their fault. It was the fault of whoever it was that had started it all.

Richard followed him, waiting for Timothy to speak. When he didn't, Richard nodded. All of his team were deep thinkers. They thought through what was going on before they spoke.

"Richard? How do we do this over the next few days? We have to be away tomorrow and into the next day."

"We do. We'll work through it. Don has agreed to free up Paul and Thomas and send them here. Mae is aware of it. So is Tate. She's not going to be happy until this is over."

"That is true. And then she'll just walk away." Timothy drew in a deep quivering breath and walked down the steps and across the street.

Richard watched him go, sorrow in his heart for his friend. He looked up, simply asking for protection for his friends and peace in what they faced.

Mae watched Tate closely, knowing that Tate was stressed and was becoming brittle.

"Tate? What do you want to do tonight?" Mae simply waited for Tate to respond.

Tate shrugged, unable to trust her voice.

"I don't know, Mae. I don't want to stay here but I have nowhere else to go."

"You're not going anywhere. Now, tomorrow? Let's plan on shopping. You need some more clothes and I could use some new summer shirts." Mae rose, reaching to pull Tate up and into a hug. "Right now? Our company has left. I think a simple supper and an early night for both of us."

The next day, Tate moved through the downtown area, Mae beside her. She still felt afraid but was determined to keep on with her life. She knew that Paul and Thomas, introduced to her that morning, were trailing them, their eyes on the crowd around them.

"Are we really safe?" Tate was feeling more and more afraid.

"I think so. You don't, though, do you?" Mae pulled her into a small shop, waving at the owner as she walked to the back.

"No, I don't. Someone is out there, Mae. I just want this over and over now."

"We know that you do. Here, we're done. We'll head home and lock ourselves in." Mae glanced at her watch. "It's late afternoon. We'll call Bill or Lily or Andrew and let them know that we're at home and safe."

"Okay. Paul and Thomas are here?"

"They are. They're staying until tomorrow when Richard's team is back. Now, let's head home." Mae waited patiently for Tate to move.

Tate stopped in her tracks, finally understanding what Mae was saying. She turned, happiness on her face.

"Mae? Is that really true? This is my home?"

"It is, Tate. It is. We don't want you to leave ever." She hugged her friend and then pointed to the back door. "Come on, girl. Out that door and then home."

Paul and Thomas walked the perimeter of the yard and then took up their spots where they planned to spend the night. They would take turns on guard but that was something that they had done many times in the past.

Timothy watched the road flying by the van the next morning. They were on their way home, another successful task behind him. He turned to Richard, finding Richard watching him.

"Richard? Have you ever thought of doing what Abe does?"

"You mean training?" Richard waited for Timothy to nod, his eyes catching the looks of interest on the faces of the other three. "I have. We need to think about this and pray about it. Don's on board as well. If and when we marry, we don't want to be traveling and away for days on end. Timothy, I think you're starting something for our group. We don't know where you stand with Tate and she needs to hear that from you first. Whatever you decide, we back you. That's how it is. We're praying for you, my friend." He looked towards the front of the van, Stephen's hands steady on the wheel. "Get us home, Stephen. Timothy has someone that he needs to find."

Chapter 41

Tate walked into Timothy's arms, reaching to hug him. She turned her face up to his, surprised when he kissed her. He bit at his lip after he did so. He hadn't meant to do that, not yet.

"Tate? Are you up to a meal out tonight?" Timothy waited, knowing that he would do whatever it was that Tate felt safe doing.

"I am. Are we safe?" Tate was still very worried.

"As safe as we can be. I am tired of hiding, Tate. I want to be seen around town with my lady. We haven't been able to do so."

"Your lady?" Tate stared at him. "Where does that come from?"

"It's how I see you, Tate. As my lady. We need to speak, but just let me say that I do love you. I have no idea how you feel. We've been in such a turmoil since we met. We need to get to know one another without running for our lives."

Tate suddenly glowed, a huge smile on her face. Timothy found himself the recipient of a hard hug before Tate danced away. She turned back.

"How dressy?"

"How dressy? For tonight, I think casual. However, once this is over, I want to take you out on a dressy date. Game for that?" He grinned as she flew back into his arms.

"I am. Okay. So where do we eat?" Tate waited for him to close the car door after her, watching as he walked around the car to slide behind the wheel.

"I think Ev's if that works." He knew that Avery, Andrew's cousin who worked in federal law enforcement, was there that evening, working with his mother, Ev.

"That's fine. Madigan took me there one day. Their food is good." She bit at her lip. "Your trip? It went okay?"

"It did, thanks for asking. It was good to be home." Timothy waited for Tate to speak. "What happened, Tate?"

"Mae and I were downtown yesterday. I didn't feel safe. There was someone following us. I didn't see anything. Paul and Thomas said that they didn't either. That makes me think that it's someone here in town."

"It is. I spoke briefly with Bill. They are ready to serve the warrants tonight. They are hoping to arrest everyone tonight. He just asked that we take precautions until they get to us that everyone involved is in jail."

Tate stood by Timothy's vehicle at Ev's, not moving. Her eyes were on the man and woman who stood behind Timothy. A weapon had appeared in the man's hand, directed at Timothy's head. She was afraid to speak, afraid to move.

Timothy kept his eyes steady on Tate. He didn't know if there was anyone around who could or would help them. He didn't know who was behind him. He hadn't been able to see before the weapon had appeared and Tate had frozen in place.

"You're coming with us. Move. Now."

Tate reached for the hand that Timothy extended, her hand cold and shaking. *This is is, isn't it, Lord? This is where we die. I don't see anyone who can help us.*

Timothy walked confidently towards the vehicle waiting, catching movement out of the corner of his eyes. He didn't know if the person was friend or foe. His whole concentration was on Tate and ensuring that she came to no harm.

Stopping by the vehicle, Timothy simply waited. He had no intention of getting into it. He watched the couple before nodding. *Yes,* he thought to himself, *these are the ones. The ones who have been after us. They are prominent in town but are not that well liked. Their history has been too shady as they say.*

"In!" The man poked at Timothy with his weapon, angry that Timothy wasn't moving. He didn't see the men moving in behind him. His whole concentration was on Timothy and Tate. "I said, get in!"

Timothy moved Tate behind him and backed them away from the car, with careful slow steps. The man followed them, angry words spewing from his mouth. The woman tottered after them on her high heels, obviously having taken too much alcohol before they appeared.

Bill and Lily shared a look and then walked towards the couple. Lily's hands reached to grasp the woman's wrists, handcuffs locked in place. She ignored her screeches to leave her alone.

Approaching the man, Bill simply reached for the man's wrist. His hard grasp caused the man to drop the weapon and Bill kicked it to one side. Handcuffs were snapped in place on his wrists as well before Bill shoved him towards the patrol officers who surrounded them.

Timothy wrapped Tate into his arms, tightening them as he felt her shuddering. He dropped a kiss on the top of her head, whispering a prayer in her ear.

"Can't you two stay out of trouble?" Bill gave a quick grin at them.

"We're trying, Bill. It's everyone else who seems to think that we need to be involved in problems. Are they the final ones?"

Bill nodded, turning to scan the crowd who had gathered. He frowned for a moment and was then away, approaching a couple who stood in the midst. He spoke quietly to them and then beckoned Lily over. She disappeared with the couple.

Tate watched with a frown before she gave a small sound. She reached to rub at her eyes.

"Tate? My love? Are you okay?" Timothy's gaze shifted between where Bill stood and the woman in his arms.

"That was my parents. What are they doing here? I haven't seen them for so long. What is going on?" Tate turned to hug him, feeling his arms tighten around her.

"Bill?" Timothy's voice was quiet but full of questions.

"Tate. Your parents are here. We've taken them in to question them. We won't let them near you until we are sure that they don't mean you any harm. And only if and when you want to see them. You get to make that decision. Not anyone else. You and Timothy. Let's get your statements and then get you home."

Timothy sighed, knowing that their date had just disappeared.

"Thanks, Bill. We were planning on eating here, but I don't think we're all that hungry at the moment."

"No, I don't expect that you are. Ev will have something that you can take home with you. And then we'll talk. I mean that, Tate. We will talk. Give u a day or so and then we'll meet with everyone.

Chapter 42

Tate snuggled down tight to Timothy, his arms around her. It was three days later and they had all gathered in Mae's home. They had shared a meal, a time of prayer, and were now waiting for the police detectives to give the final update on their investigation. She looked around at all her friends that were there, new friends who had simply taken her into their hearts. She was thankful for them. God had blessed her richly, she decided.

Timothy stared down at Tate before he looked over at Bill, who was conferring with Lily and Richard. He sighed. *This is it, isn't it, Lord? This is where we find out the why's of it all. I don't know that we have all the answers though. Something tells me that we don't. I fear for my team. If it follows as it did with others of our friends, then these four will have life and death situations. And I don't want that for them.*

Bill turned at last, reaching for the folders that he had set aside when he entered the house. He searched the faces of those gathered, stopping as he reached Tate and Timothy. They were a couple, he thought, and needed this closure.

"Tate? Your parents? They were not involved in all this. I'm sorry that you were put through what you have been for the last ten years. It shouldn't have happened. They didn't realize that when they asked you to leave, that you really would and literally move from your home province. They did hire someone to search for you and follow you when they could. They just wanted to make sure that you were safe."

"They could have approached me." Tate didn't want to meet with them. "I don't want to meet them, at least not yet, if that's what you're not asking."

"They do want to meet with you. They have returned to your home province, leaving a letter for you that they have asked that you read at some point. They understand that you have been deeply hurt. They have no explanation other than that they were trying to have you learn to stand on your own feet."

"That's a strange way to do things." Tate wrapped her hands around Timothy's, finding his warm on hers.

"It is. Now, as to what was happening? The couple that tried to abduct you three days ago?"

"Them? Who are they?" Tate turned to look up at Timothy.

"They were prominent in town, Tate. He was a businessman, deep into crime. He was a financial advisor, Tate. His wife didn't work but she spent more than he seemed to take in. It is obvious that they didn't have the means to live as they had been. It has become obvious now that they were living on the proceeds of crime. They had you kidnapped Tate and brought here. Why they went after Timothy, they are not saying other than someone asked them to. The house where you were kept Timothy? It belongs to their company. They had added your parents's name, Tate, to their company's paperwork without their consent or knowledge. The wife, Judy Taylor, is from your home province. She has admitted that she knew your parents in school. She had a grudge against them because they had you and she couldn't have any children. Her husband, Ted, has refused to talk. Their workers are talking, giving more and more details."

"I don't understand why. It has to be more than just a grudge." Tate looked around Timothy at Richard as he looked up from his phone.

"I know why, Tate. It's not pretty. Your grandparents and hers had been in business together at one time. Your grandparents pulled back from them when hers turned to crime. They walked away from that business and set up a rival business, which did much better than her grandparents'."

"Now, that makes sense. So she has been resentful all these years for many reasons and decided that I needed to pay? But that doesn't explain Timothy."

"No, it doesn't. The only explanation that they could provide is that someone wanted Timothy destroyed and they thought this would do it. They have no other reasoning for this. And they can't provide any other information on that."

"What about David?" Timothy had not seen his old friend for a while and that concerned him.

Bill grew more sober.

"I'm sorry, Timothy. Patrick saw you two talking, approached him, and then killed him. He had somehow discovered who David worked for and couldn't take a chance that you two would speak."

Timothy's eyes slid shut. David had been a good friend to him. Now he was gone. He would find David's family somehow and do what he could for them.

Tate grew silent, not hearing the buzz of conversation around her. Timothy simply held her, ready for whatever emotion that she showed. It finally grew quiet as their friends left.

Mae turned on the lights as dusk grew, closing the drapes. She paused, her eyes on the young couple, before she moved to the kitchen. They needed to eat, only she didn't know how much they would feel like eating.

"Okay, my love?" Timothy's voice broke through the silence.

"I think so. I'm getting there. How about you?" She looked up at him, finding his eyes on her, eyes that were full of love just for her. "Timothy?"

"We'll talk, my love. We'll talk. Tonight it's enough that we're safe and we can start a life together."

"A life together?" Tate stared at him before she stepped back. "We'll see, Timothy. For now, I think Mae has a meal for us." She walked away from him, a little skip in her step.

Timothy smiled, knowing that Tate was the lady for him. He looked up, thanking God for bringing them together. They had not faced what others had but He had brought them through it all.

Her hand tight in Timothy's, Tate drew in a deep breath of summer air. They were walking through a park near the edge of town, one that they favoured. They had shared a meal at Ev's and then headed. Timothy and Tate had been dating for the last three months, spending as much time together as they could. She looked up at him, her heart on her face. She had learned to be open with him. Her friends in town had simply enveloped her into their group and she enjoyed their company.

"Timothy? When do you head out again?" Tate worried about him every time they left.

"Tomorrow. We're gone for three days which will feel like three years. I don't want to go." Timothy reached to kiss her. "I miss you when we're apart."

"I know that you do. I miss you as well."

Timothy pointed to a bench. "Let's have a seat, my love." Once they were seated, Timothy simply wrapped her into his arms. "Have you thought any more about talking with your parents?"

"I'm still praying about it. Madigan and I are talking. She's giving me good counsel on that. Silas has been part of our talks. I'm not sure that I will or that I can. I have too much baggage regarding them. I still haven't read their letter. I'm not sure when I'll be able to."

"That's understandable. You were put through a lot by others and they didn't help. They asked you to leave without explaining why. That broke your trust in them. It takes time to heal, if it ever does."

"It does." Tate grew pensive, not watching Timothy as he fidgeted for a moment.

"Tate?" Timothy waited until she turned to him. "We haven't known each other for that long, but I love you. I love you more than I thought that I could ever love anyone. I was so afraid that I would lose you or that you would walk away. Will you marry me, be my sweetheart for life?"

Tate stared at him, tears momentarily blinding her. She sniffed, trying to control her emotions.

"Timothy, you have no idea how I have prayed for someone like you. Yes, I love you. I will marry you." She reached for his kiss and then watched as he placed a ring with a ruby stone on her finger.

"We don't need to rush into our marriage, my love. Mae took me aside the other day, asking when I would ask you and then telling me that you had a home with her as long as you wanted. You're not losing her. She's just across the street from me."

"I know. I would be sad to lose her. She's become like a mother or an older sister to me. It shows me how much I missed out during my life. My mother was very reserved and I thought that was how it should be."

"And Mom and Dad are there for you. Mom worries about you, wanting just to smother you."

"Your family is priceless. And I love your little nephew."

———

They grew quiet, content in their love for one another and content in their trust and faith in God. He had protected them and brought them through their adventure. Their faith had grown and for that they were grateful for their adventure. Neither one thought that their faith would be as strong as it would have been otherwise.

Dear Readers:

Thank you for choosing to read the story of Timothy and his lady love, Tate. I had not planned on telling the story of Richard and his team of four. They had other ideas. As I was working through the series of *His Ladies with The Lamps*, they became more and more visible and more and more vocal that they had stories to tell. And of course, I did have to oblige them.

Tate and Timothy's faith was tested in many ways. They had to learn to trust God in new ways, understanding that He would never leave them or forsake them. He was their Protector in many ways.

As we go through life, we each face difficulties and adversity. We are not alone. Just as God was with these two, He is with us. I cling to the promises that we are not alone, that He loves us so much, and that He does protect us.

As to the teams that were mentioned, Abe's team's stories are in *His Guardians*. Don's team is mimicking Richard, his team of six telling me that each man has a story to tell. We'll see what happens there. As to the others who are mentioned? Bill and Cora's story is *Hidden in the Hollow*. Silas and Madigan's is *Strong Courage*. Andrew and Phoebe's is *The Potter's Hands*. Samuel and Aideen and that group of friends have their stories told in *His Warriors*.

God bless each one of you.

Ronna

Website: www.ronnabacon.com

9 781998 821037